A Man Dead

A Man Dead

To Kill A Man, Book Three

Stuart G. Yates

Also by Stuart G. Yates

- Unflinching

- In The Blood

- To Die in Glory

- Varangian

- Varangian 2 (King of the Norse)

- Burnt Offerings

- Whipped Up

- Splintered Ice

- The Sandman Cometh

- Roadkill

- Tears in the Fabric of Time

- Sallowed Blood

- Lament for Darley Dene

- The Pawnbroker

- Bloody Reasons (To Kill A Man Book 1)

- Pursuers Unto Death (to Kill A Man Book 2)

Also by Stuart G. Yates

1

Reining in his horse, Bart Stenton gazed out across the prairie before closing his eyes and taking a deep breath. He loved this land. He loved the loneliness of it, the wild, unsullied beauty, the endless rolling plain, the distant hills shrouded in light purple mist. Once, not so very long ago, countless savages roamed this place, hearts filled with hatred, minds set on violence. But years of determined killing had removed the threat. Now, all was peaceful, apart from the occasional war band, groups of stinking, starving, godless warriors, all of whom he enjoyed hunting and butchering.

He knew that soon, no such pleasurable pursuits would punctuate his life. The tribes were gradually being pushed away from populated areas and forced into reservations. With this containment, the sport of killing would end. He knew it would happen, but not yet. He hoped, not yet. He was an Indian-fighter, adept at killing, be it close-up and face-to-face or from a distance. He didn't mind which, so long as another red-skinned sonofabitch lay bloody and dead on the ground. It was all the same to Bart Stenton.

Following the course of the river, he led his horse to one of the locations he knew well, where the grass grew lush and succulent. He jumped down from the saddle and stretched out his back, allowing his horse to chomp noisily and fill its belly with nature's goodness. Drifting down to the river bank, he got down on his knees, splashed water over his face and reached for his canteen to refill it.

He stopped, senses alert, as he heard something. The sound, faint but distinct, of a human being. A stifled moan of someone in pain. Careful now, Stenton settled his canteen down on the ground and eased his Remington revolver from its holster. He waited, listening for another sound, anxious to get his bearings.

It came. Prolonged. The definite groan of a man in agony.

Moving stealthily along the grassy banks, he headed in the direction of the sound. His moccasin-clad feet barely broke the blades of grass he walked on. With each step, the sound grew louder. Unmistakable. Rhythmical. Constant.

Crouching down, he carefully parted the tall grass and took in the scene before him. For a moment, he stared, confused and speechless. He couldn't quite believe what he saw, so he pressed finger and thumb into his eyes, shook his head vigorously and looked again.

There was no mistaking what he was witnessing.

A naked savage, his sweat-soaked body rippling with passion and muscle, had a poor, helpless white boy pinned to the ground. This boy, also naked, arms held down high above his head, writhed in agony underneath the vile redskin, who ploughed his large manhood repeatedly into the forbidden nether regions of the young man's body. Such a scene belonged in the very bowels of hell itself.

Disgusted, his stomach gripped with the urge to vomit, Stenton rose to his feet and, all caution pushed aside, strode out into open view.

The savage saw him and ceased his thrusting. Something flickered across his face. Alarm. Terror. Total bewilderment. He pulled back and the young man cried out as the redskin's still erect manhood slipped free of his despoiled body. The redskin's hands came up, his mouth opened, the first words of protest and surrender formed on his lips. But no sound came out.

Stenton shot him, the heavy caliber slug slamming into the Indian's chest, sending him reeling backwards. He squawked in pain and fear, tried to lever himself back up, and Stenton shot him again, the bullet striking him in the right collarbone. Stenton advanced and, with each step, he put another slug into the filthy savage's body, perforating his loathsome flesh with lead.

Six shots spent, Stenton, standing over the barely breathing savage, cracked open the cylinder and spilled the cartridges into the ground. He fed in six more bullets, and emptied the revolver into the savage with evenly spaced shots. Only then did he stop, lower the smoking hand gun and, eyes closed, utter a silent prayer skywards.

"Oh, sweet Jesus," came a small voice from behind him.

Stenton whirled to see the young man trembling before him, hands clasped over his groin to hide the shame of his nakedness, his body lily-white in the glare of the morning sun.

"It's all right, son," said Stenton. Dropping the gun into its holster, he put a fatherly arm protectively around the young man's shoulders. "It's all over now."

Breaking down, the young man pressed himself into Stenton's chest, his sobs loud and strong. Stenton, basking in the righteousness of his actions, patted the young man's head and smiled. This was already a good day and it had barely begun.

2

A buzzard circled overhead, its occasional screech ringing out across the endless reaches of the cloudless sky. As he sat on the buckboard, reins looped lightly through his fingers, Han watched the bird intently, knowing its presence was a bad omen. Behind him, huddled beneath a threadbare blanket, the woman stirred restlessly. They had spent the best part of two days in a fruitless search for her boy, taken by a Comanche raiding party. She'd pleaded, *begged* him to continue, but it was useless. Han was no tracker, so they packed up the open wagon and headed south towards a small mining town in the hope of finding his sister.

"You expect me to help you, when you do *nothing* for me!" she had yelled, beating her fists against his chest. She blamed the Okinawan for everything, regardless of the facts, her hatred for him boundless. The Indians attacked her homestead in the night, ghostly shapes in the dark, and they killed both her man and Han's companion. They had taken her son, Jeremiah.

"They'll murder him!" she had cried, slumping down in the dirt to wail and rock herself backwards and forwards.

The search would always be fruitless. Han told her so. She didn't listen, just kept on crying and rocking, her mind and body racked with grief. He waited, sitting in silence next to her, staring out into the dull, grey morning after the attack had been beaten back. Han had killed many of them, but not enough.

At last, sitting up straight, her shoulders heaving, she grew quiet. "What will they do to him? Scalp him, and then what? Torture?"

"No. They will keep him and feed him so that he grows strong and straight."

"You don't know that."

"It is what they do. They do it many times. They use their seed and replenish their family stock. Girls, to carry offspring."

"Holy Christ! And you think that is better than killing him? They'll use him as breeding stock, like a goddamned animal?"

"In the years to come, he will forget who he was. He will think it natural for him to find a woman from the tribe to have a family with."

"You heathen bastard. You're as cold and as heartless as they are. Dear God, you even *look* like them!"

He turned away. "I did not make this country what it is. You cannot blame me for its ways, its evil. I came here believing it was a good place, full of opportunities. Instead, all I have found is sadness and bitterness. Lies and betrayal." He looked at her. "Do you not think that if I could, I would undo everything? Of course I would. If I had known what lay waiting for us, like a thief in the night, I would have stayed in my home and never urged my family to come to this damned place. You are not the only one who has lost loved ones."

For a long time, her eyes studied his face. She didn't say anything more, but Han knew her hatred for him continued to simmer away just under the surface.

They moved away in the general direction of the town she'd called Prairie Rise. They hoped they might be able to rustle up some help... perhaps convince the Army to send a troop to track down the raiders who had taken her son. Perhaps. But the town held bitter memories for her. It was there that the gunfighter, John Wesley Hardin, had killed her husband. Nobody cared about that. Why should they care about her son?

They camped by a stream that first evening. The air was thick, the heat oppressive and, as the sun went down, Han stripped off his shirt and pants and swam in the cool water. She stood on the bank and watched him. Her eyes never left him as he stepped out from the water and stood before her, drying himself off with an old blanket from the back of the wagon.

"Okinawan," she said quietly. He stopped, pressing the coarse material of the blanket against his face. He frowned. "What is that? The name of a tribe?"

He let slip a small, sharp laugh. "What is your name? You have not told me your name."

"Susannah. Suzie for short."

"My name is Han."

"I'm not interested in your name, nor anything to do with you."

Grunting, Han dried himself and pulled on his shirt. He sat down next to the small fire he'd made. Susannah made pancakes and fried them in an old tin plate. They ate in silence.

"Why did you lead those murdering bastards to our home?"

She spoke with as much indifference as if she were asking him the time. He stared at her, incredulous. How could she turn so sharply? So suddenly?

He wiped his plate with the last piece of his food and munched it down. "I didn't."

"Strange how they appeared almost as soon as you did."

"Do you truly believe what you say?" Shaking his head, he threw his plate to the ground. "Think about it, for one second, eh? I lead them to your place, then kill them when they attack. What would be the point in that?"

"Maybe you changed your mind. Maybe you saw something you liked." She arched a single eyebrow, the light from the fire picking out and contorting her features, making her appear almost maniacal in the orange glow. "I've seen the way you look at me with your eyes full of lust."

He turned away, feeling hot, and not only from the fire.

"You can't deny it. You heathens are all the same – after one thing and one thing alone. Tell me it isn't so."

But he couldn't, because he knew it was true.

3

Sitting astride an ancient fallen tree trunk, Ritter, lost in the cleaning of his revolver, did not notice Nati's approach until she was almost upon him. Turning to her, he smiled into her smooth, handsome face. She pushed back his hat and planted a kiss on his lips, her left hand gripping the hair at the nape of his neck. Responding, he looped his arm around her waist, moaning at the taste and feel of her.

"You hungry?" she asked, pulling away and sitting down.

"For you I am."

She sniggered, tapping his lips with a forefinger. "You're a terrible man, Gus Ritter. You need your wits about you, and your strength. The good Father says we're less than a day away from the next big town."

"What's that got to do with anything?" He leaned into her and kissed her again.

Pushing him back with her palms, she grinned. "Well, because when we get there, we can get ourselves a room."

"A room?"

"Yes. A girl wants a bit of luxury now and then. My body's all battered and bruised with rolling around on this dusty dry earth every time we do it." She stomped the ground to give emphasis to her words. "I want crisp, clean bed sheets and deep-piled pillows. That's how a gentleman treats a lady, Gus Ritter."

"I ain't no gentleman," he said and made a grab for her.

Giggling, she jumped up and danced out of reach. "Don't I know it!"

"You ain't complained so far."

She feigned a blush, hand clamped to her mouth, eyes averted. "My, you are a *scoundrel*. If I didn't think better, I'd say you was a—"

"When you two love-birds have quite finished," came Father Merry's voice, as he crossed from the camp-fire towards them, "dinner is served."

Sighing, Gus fed six cartridges into his gun's cylinder whilst Nati skipped away, laughing. "I thought you was on watch?"

"I was," said the priest, and he sat down. "But there ain't anyone out here, Gus. We're a day away from Saint Angelo. This time tomorrow, we can replenish our stores, ask around and get our bearings."

"A day away, or even five minutes away, this area is still dangerous." He stood up. "I'll scout around."

"There's no need, Gus."

"There's always the need, padre."

He moved off, raising his hand to Nati as she helped Grace ladle out the last of the bean stew.

"Don't you want some?" called Grace, dragging her forearm across her brow.

"Later," he said, and quickly moved on, not wishing either of the two ladies to notice the pained expression he knew he sported. The thought of yet another helping of beans and axle grease was too much to stomach. Nati's description of a comfortable hotel room steered his mind towards imagining a good dinner of steak, potatoes and rich gravy – a thought so good, he could almost taste it!

He climbed to the top of a sharp ridge and settled himself down to scan the surroundings. Mainly composed of rock and clumps of gorse, the plain was of a uniform grey colour, slightly undulating, disappearing towards distant, smoky mountains.

Narrowing his eyes, he focused in on one area. From here, it was difficult to estimate the distance, but it must have been at least half a day's ride away. His attention was grabbed by a thin trail of smoke which blended in with the mountain backdrop, making it difficult to see with any real clarity. But smoke it was, of that he was certain. Caused by what, however, was another matter. It might have been burning grassland. The area tinder dry, the merest spark enough to set undergrowth ablaze. Or, just as easily, it could have been a homestead, attacked and burned, as so many were.

The culprits were usually Comanches, but any number of other tribes could be the perpetrators. This was a brutal land, but it was home to the Comanche and they, together with their native brothers, were fighting for their very existence in the face of constant and relentless expansion west by the white man.

Something moved over to his right. Flattening himself against the rock, he peered across to where the area rose in jagged, pointing fingers, like the one on which he himself was perched, some twenty or so feet skywards. He waited, holding his breath, forcing himself not to blink.

There it was again.

A definite shape, scurrying between the crags.

Cursing himself for not bringing a rifle, he carefully drew his revolver. A shot from this distance would be useless, but it might draw whoever, or whatever, it was from cover.

It moved again, revealing itself at last.

A man. Dressed in buckskin leggings, torso naked, rifle in hand. Blue-black hair hung down to his shoulders, the top like a thatch, festooned with a pair of bright feathers.

He recognized the garb and the adornments and his stomach flipped.

Comanche.

They were already under attack when he bounded down from his look-out position. Tricking him by drawing his attention to the lone warrior amongst the rocks, as the rest of the raiding party hit them from the rear. Ritter ran, bent double, arms and legs pumping. He knew if he made it to the wagon, he could seize a rifle, put these sonsofbitches in the ground.

He saw Merry, held by the throat, one of them at his front, a second with his naked legs wrapped around him, forcing him to the ground. Merry was a big man. He'd already killed one of them and the redskin lay sprawled out at his feet, eyes wide open, staring into nothing. But there were too many. Beyond the priest, a warrior back-handed Grace to the ground, while Nati lashed out and hurled the pot of bean stew into the face of another attacker. He screamed, falling backwards, hands clamped over his face, and Nati swept up the warrior's rifle, worked the lever and put a bullet through yet another of them who appeared from the surrounding rocks.

Ritter's gun barked in his hands. He shot two of them. Whether they fell dead or not, he didn't care. He raced on, smacking a Comanche across the face with his gun, then made it to the wagon. Ripping away the flap, he took the Winchester and turned in time to confront a Comanche charging towards him, hatchet held aloft. Ritter rammed the rifle stock into the Indian's face, stepped forward and began to pump bullets into the others.

All around him the wild whooping of the attacking warriors. Their blood lust up, determined to kill, no matter what. Ritter saw Nati – saw the warrior on her, his knife flashing. Then the blood. He groaned, not wanting to witness this, not wishing to believe this was how it was all going to end.

Grace screamed. Whirling, Ritter put two bullets into the back of a Comanche's head, but even then, he knew he was too late. Walking at a steady pace, he shot Nati's attacker. She was alive, the knife having scraped across her forearm. Backed up against the rocks, she was holding onto the deep gash as blood seeped between her fingers. A look flashed between them. "Gus!" she shouted in warning and he responded, spinning around bent double, and put several shots into a screaming Comanche killer closing on him.

Across to his right, a hatchet flashed and he watched, transfixed, as Merry went down, hand raised in a pathetic attempt to parry the blow. Ritter shuddered at the sound of axe cutting into flesh.

A warrior rose naked from where Grace lay in a dishevelled mess, his member collapsing after his exertions. Forgetting about using bullets, Ritter strode over to him and broke his skull like an egg with a violent swing of the rifle's stock.

He looked down.

Grace was dead, her throat slit, the blood still gurgling from the gaping wound.

For a moment, he almost lost his senses. The strength drained from his legs and he fell against a nearby boulder, holding onto it, gulping down air. Shaking, he turned again towards the priest and his assailant, in the act of finishing the padre off with another axe blow. Ritter shot the Comanche through the head.

It was over.

The last few Comanche warriors disappeared amongst the rocks, leaving their dead and dying behind. They wanted the horses and whatever supplies they could take. Instead, all they received was the death of half a dozen of their band. A heavy price to have paid for failure.

Except in the killing of more white people.

"Oh, dear God, Gus."

He looked up and saw Nati, clutching her arm now tightly wrapped in a bandana, edging towards Grace. She fell to her knees and burst into tears.

Ritter turned away, unable to face the reality. Grace, dead. Perhaps Merry, too. The man who knew where John Wesley Hardin was to be found. The reason why Ritter was here in the first place. All of it such a waste.

He slid down the rock and fell on his backside.

And he wept.

Nati did the best she could, tending Merry's wounds with the last few drops of their water supply. He lay in a quivering heap, the hatchet wounds deep and vicious-looking. She softened hunks of bread by chewing them, then pressed the pulp into the wounds before dressing them with strips of cloth torn from one of Ritter's shirts. Every few seconds, she'd stop, head hanging, sucking in breath, the cut on her arm throbbing as if it were alive.

Meanwhile, Ritter dug a shallow grave for Grace. Part of him suspected the Comanches would return to desecrate her resting place in revenge for what had happened, but he pushed such thoughts aside. He had to do something… had to bring some decency to this whole sorry mess, even if only temporarily.

Later, they laid Merry in the wagon and set off once more on the trail.

"We're a day out from the next town, is what the padre said." Ritter looked at Nati. "Do you think he'll make it?"

"He is strong. If anyone can, he can."

Turning his gaze to her wound, he wondered if the same might be said about her. He'd seen wounded men die from such a cut. If it turned bad… He shuddered and looked again at the trail snaking ahead of them. "Then we must make every moment count. Just in case."

She stroked the loaded Winchester lying across her lap and grunted her agreement.

4

The door creaked open and the Captain looked up from the telegram he was reading through for the third time. In front of him, the young Lieutenant saluted, rigid, mechanical, like one of those new-fangled clockwork toys he'd seen for sale in Boston. "At ease, son," he snapped.

He waved the paper. "This came through from Laramie. Damn territory is alive with marauding Comanch. They're raiding farms and homesteads right down into New Mexico. Seems they don't much like the idea of living in a reservation, so they're doing their damndest to replenish their horse herd and keep themselves on the move. They have been spotted near Saint Angelo. A nearby farmer took the news to Archangel and wired us this." He slapped the telegram onto his desk.

"I assume you want me to go and find out the truth, sir?"

"I *want* you to find this raiding party and put an end to it, that's what I want, Lieutenant. If they attack the railroad at Prairie Rise and hold up the building work, the Governor will have my hide. It's all about dollars and cents, Connick. Nothing more."

"And the lives of the settlers, sir, surely?"

"Shoot, Lieutenant, grow up! I know you enlisted in the cavalry for all the right reasons, the moral side of it, upholding justice, and the rights of the common citizen and all that hocus pocus, but the truth is, it's big business which dictates what we do. That's why we're here, son. No other reason. We protect the railroad and we do so by killing redskins. So, you put your noble aspirations to one side and ready your company, Lieutenant. I want you provisioned, saddled up and gone by tomorrow first light. Dismissed."

Connick brought his heels together and saluted. He spun round and took a step towards the door.

"And don't come back until the job is done, you hear me? I don't want no bureaucrat from Washington down here telling me I didn't do my job."

Pulling in a breath, Connick stared at his commanding officer. "Meaning what, sir?"

"Meaning, bring me evidence, boy. That's what I mean."

"Evidence, sir? I don't quite understand what you—"

"You bring me their goddamned fucking scalps, get me?"

For a moment, it looked as if Connick was about to topple over in a dead faint.

"Captain Jewson, sir, I'm not sure if the men will—"

"The men will do as they are ordered, Connick." The Captain leaned across his desk, pressing his knuckles down hard on the surface. "Maybe it's you that can't. Or won't."

Bringing his heels together again, Connick jutted out his chest. "If those *are* your orders, sir, I will obey."

"Damned right you will. Dismissed, Lieutenant."

The door banged shut and Jewson flopped down in his chair. He picked up the telegram and read it through once more. Sighing, he screwed it up into a tight ball and hurled it into the corner of his small, stuffy office. Then he pulled out a desk drawer and brought out the bottle of bourbon he kept in there for moments such as these. Without bothering to find a glass, he took a long drink from the bottle then, smacking his lips, leaned back and looked at the ceiling. "Dear Lord, don't let them come back." Then he closed his eyes and tried to blank it all from his mind.

An hour or so later, there came a tentative rap on the office door. Jewson, in a half-sleep, flickered open his eyes and grunted, "Come."

A brash-looking, round, squat Warrant Officer stepped inside, clutching his hat in both hands, eyes flitting around the room. "I've just seen Connick at the head of a troop. They've gone."

"Thank God for that. I thought at one point he'd refuse."

"Do we leave now?"

"No, Oscar, not just yet." He gestured towards the bottle. "Sit down and have a drink. We'll leave early morning, before the day has started. I'll tell the guards at the gate we're going across to Angelo to deliver a message to the marshal there."

"But there isn't any marshal there."

Jewson gave him a look. "Just sit down, you ass."

Oscar did so and watched, licking his lips, as Jewson poured him a drink. "You think they got the shipment?"

"I expect so. Damn it, there's enough of them."

Sipping the bourbon, Oscar closed his eyes. "I hope this works, Franklyn, I really do."

"It will. We've been planning it for long enough. Look," he leaned forward, his hard stare locked onto Oscar's face, "this is no time to be getting cold feet. We meet them where we arranged, they give us the money, and that's the end of it." He raised his own glass. "Until next time."

"Shoot, Franklyn, I don't want there to be a next time."

"Twenty thousand dollars ain't going to buy us a lifetime of luxury, Oscar. If we can do it two more times, I reckon we can retire."

"Shoot." He shook his head, staring into the contents of his glass. "That's thirty-thousand each."

"Exactly. Now," he topped up the Warrant Officer's glass, "drink up. It's a two-day ride to the meet. You're gonna need all your strength."

5

Toby's head lolled from side to side, the horse carrying him mindless of its rider's condition. It stomped and plodded along as it carelessly negotiated the many ruts and pot-holes, but Toby slept on regardless, in complete exhaustion.

They'd found him in the stable, propped in the corner. The young stable-hand turned his terrified eyes towards Reece striding towards him. He started trying to explain, but Reece still shot him through the heart.

Ordering the others to carry Toby's dead-weight to the horse, Reece shook his head, barely able to contain his disgust. "I don't know why I bother."

"Because he's your brother, maybe?"

Reece turned a jaundiced eye towards his top ranch-hand. "Willis, be he my brother or not – which, in all accuracy of blood and ancestry and all, he truly is not – the only reason I'm saving his sorry ass is so he can lead me to that murdering bastard, Father Merry. He killed my father, my true brother also. I'll not let that stand."

"And when you've killed Merry, what then?"

"I aim to split his balls before I hang him by his tongue, that's what I aim to do."

"Even so, the question still stands. What then?"

Tilting his head, Reece regarded his foreman with a quizzical look. "What are you getting at?"

"Mr Reece, sir, I don't wish to sound disrespectful or nothing, but—"

"Say what you have to say, goddammit."

"Well, I worked for your father nigh on twenty years and his death was a terrible blow to me, I'll tell you that much."

"His murder, you mean."

"Yessir, I do, but regardless, I know how much he put into his ranch, how he worked so hard to have something to pass onto his boys – meaning you and Mr Mario, sir."

"Well, Mario is dead, done for by that bastard Merry."

"Yessir, which is my point. You is so fixed on killing that damned priest, you ain't looking to what will happen after. Now that Mr Mario is gone, poor old Toby is the only kin you've got. I reckon you should be looking after him, making sure he survives the journey to wherever it is we're heading."

Now, as Reece rode beside his brutalized half-brother, Willis's wise words rang home. Reece reached across to check the binding which prevented Toby from slipping out of the saddle. Satisfied, he turned his gaze towards the trail they followed. None too concerned if Toby died or not, the words of his foreman caused him to consider the future. What would happen to the ranch now that everyone was dead? Toby was the most incompetent wrangler Reece believed he'd ever seen, more interested in drinking himself half-stupid, than breaking mustangs or branding steers. He was in no doubt the fat slob would continue the same way after Reece took charge, so what was the point in offering him anything? He was worse than useless, more of a burden than anything else.

Toby may well be the fruit of his father's loins, but old Silas Scrimshaw had never married his mother. Mario and Reece alone were legitimate. It stood to reason that Reece, and Reece alone, should inherit the Scrimshaw ranch. Toby could go and rot in some run-down cantina someplace. He'd give him a handsome pay-off, but that was all. When this sorry mess was over and the priest was dead, he'd cast Toby out. To hell with him. After all, if it wasn't for Toby's thoughtless, indiscriminate use of his cock in raping that young girl, none of this would have happened. He bore the blame. The blame for everything. Perhaps, Reece considered for the umpteenth time, it should be Toby he dangled from a rope, not the priest.

And then, of course, there was Manuela, his father's mistress with whom Reece had fallen in love. A clandestine love-affair, which fell apart after old Silas's murder. The fact that Manuela's affections for his father continued to simmer still rankled with Reece. That was why they'd fought... why he'd left. When he got back, he did not believe she would be there. Life, in the space of just a few weeks, had changed out of all recognition.

"El Paso would be the logical place."

Reece looked up, his foreman's voice bringing him out of his reverie. "Eh? What's that you say? Logical? What you been doing, you old bastard, taking Sunday school lessons?"

"I have been reading, boss, yes, I'll admit it. My bones ain't as strong as they used to be and when I get home to the bunkhouse after a long day out on the range, whisky and cards don't have the same attraction they once did. So I read."

Shaking his head, Reece turned away, hawked and spat into the ground. "Shit, life truly has changed." He chuckled. "Well, when my own bones is old enough, I doubt I'll turn to books and stuff. A young, honey-skinned whore is all I'll need to ease away the aches and pains."

"If everything is still working down below."

"It will be." A sudden thought struck him and Reece arched a single eyebrow. "Don't yours?"

"Not like it used to."

"No kiddin'? Shit, I'm sorry for that, Willis, I truly am."

"To be honest, I'd much rather smoke a good cigar than roll around under the bedclothes with some wild young thing. Or," he winked, unable to contain a broad grin, "a wild old thing!"

They both laughed. Some of their companions turned quizzical gazes towards them. Reece waved them away. "So. El Paso?"

"That's where I reckon he'd head for. Nowhere else would offer him any chance of becoming invisible."

"Well, he ain't gonna be invisible to me. When I meet up with that bastard, neither his cloth nor his god is gonna be able to protect him. How far is it?"

"Best part of a week's ride, I'd say. There is a border town closer. It's called Santa Angelo, if my memory serves me right."

"All righty, then we'll head for there, ask around, see if anybody has heard anything. Who knows, it might be a good place to hole up for a little while. Stretch our legs. Find one of those honey-skinned whores, or," he gave an exaggerated wink of his own, "a fine cigar for yourself!"

And their second bout of laughter rang out across the prairie, more loudly than their first.

6

"You must be insane to think I'd allow a heathen bastard like you to come anywhere near me," she'd said when they woke up the next day.

He'd wanted to. So much. He'd watched her, mouth drooling, as she plunged into the stream, standing up to her waist, the water dripping from her bare breasts like silver beads. When she stepped clear of the water and gave him a withering look, she continued to pile on the scorn, letting him know, if he didn't already, that if such a 'godless bastard' as him thought she would ever allow his 'filthy fingers' to touch her, he'd better disappear into the night to find a coyote to lie with, because that was the best he could ever hope to find.

And so it continued both day and night as they travelled across the featureless plain, following an ancient trackway forged by pioneers a generation before them. Endless insults, the lashing of his emotions with her vicious, unforgiving tongue, until her voice became nothing more than an insect whine on the distant periphery of his hearing. He ignored her. And then, having run out of expletives and hurtful words to say, she fell silent.

He started when the bird screeched again and shot it a hateful glance. If only he was good with a rifle, he'd shoot it from the sky. It had followed them since early this morning, their third day on the trail, almost as if it knew their supplies were running low. How could it, mused Han, rolling his shoulder. Sighing, he settled his gaze straight ahead again.

The bird banked off abruptly to its right and soared out of sight. Frowning, Han reined in the horse and sat, listening. Something must have caused the bird to alter its course. Another hoped-for meal perhaps, a small animal dying from thirst. He tilted his head.

And then he heard it.

The unmistakable sound of approaching horses.

Reacting as if by a secret signal, the woman sprang up from underneath her blanket and gripped his arm. "What is it? More Indians?"

"I do not believe so," he said cautiously, all his concentration centered towards an area where the trail turned from view and disappeared amongst high, jagged rocks.

"I'll get the rifle," she said.

"No. I would not do that," he said quickly and when she stopped and looked again, she gasped.

And then she hooted with laughter.

"Dear Lord Almighty," she said and jumped down to the ground, dusting off her heavy, pleated skirt.

Han, watching the approach of a dozen or so riders, felt no such feelings of cheerful anticipation.

The men riding steadily towards them were clad in the dark blue of U.S. cavalry.

The troop reined in a few paces from the wagon and waited, their horses snorting loudly. A young officer inched forward, touching the brim of his hat towards the woman while eyeing Han suspiciously.

"I'm so happy to see you," she gushed, moving so fast towards him that the officer's mount shied away, eyes wide, nostrils flaring. She stopped, hands raised. "I'm so sorry, Captain, but I'm just so happy, so *very* happy."

"My name's Lieutenant Connick, ma'am. We're half a day's ride out from Saint Angelo, responding to reports of a Comanche war party operating in this area." Another glance towards Han. "I have to confess, I'm surprised and alarmed to find you out here in this wilderness."

"That same war party, they attacked my homestead, Captain. They killed my beloved husband and made off with my boy." Bowing her head, she sobbed, "we barely made it out alive."

A stunned silence followed. Connick recovered himself a little and shifted his weight in his saddle. "I'm shocked to hear that, ma'am." He turned around. "Sergeant Winters, approach if you would."

A large, burly-looking individual responded, together with two troopers. Drawing up close, the men all had hand weapons drawn.

"What's your name, boy?" snarled Winters, leaning forward, jutting his jaw towards Han.

"Oh, him," interjected the woman, before the Okinawan could offer a reply. "If it wasn't for him, none of this would have happened."

"I beg your pardon, ma'am?"

She turned her face towards Connick and nodded. "Oh yes. It was all his fault – he brought those heathen devils straight to our door."

Doing a double-take, Connick snapped a quizzical look towards the Okinawan.

In that brief moment, something passed between the two men and Han recognized the lieutenant's expression as the same one others had worn when he was first arrested. In a bleak, miserable place, Han, searching for his sister, was forced to defend himself from the accusations of others and, in so doing, struck out and killed. And now, here it was again. The unjustified charge of guilt, due purely to the colour of his skin.

"Hold him, Sergeant."

Winters and the two troopers moved, but Han moved faster. Launching himself from the buckboard, he kicked Winters to the ground, swung, blocked, struck, throwing one trooper over his shoulder, twisting the other's wrist to break his hold on his hand gun. Then, swivelling, he kicked Connick in the guts, doubling him over, and turned to run.

"I'll kill you, you heathen bastard."

She had a gun. In the melee, she had taken her chance, picked up Winter's Colt cavalry revolver, and held it in both hands, fully cocked. The glint in her maniacal eyes made Han realize she would shoot. So he stopped, his breath coming out in a long-drawn-out stream.

Other troopers were there now, Winchesters pointing, every one of them wary. Having seen what this little man was capable of, they kept their distance.

Heaving in a great lungful of air, Connick struggled to his feet, hands on hips, one hand clamped against his stomach. "Tie that bastard up," he wheezed, before shooting a glance towards the woman. "What sort of man is this?"

"The Comanche-loving kind."

Narrowing his eyes, the Lieutenant studied the Okinawan, turned and spat into the dirt. "Damned bastard. I'm going to enjoy seeing him dangling from the end of a rope."

"Me too, mister captain, sir," she said, lowering her gun at last and handing it back. "I'm going to have the best seat in the house."

7

He flickered open his eyes, taking a few seconds to focus himself on his surroundings. For a moment, he believed he was already dead and a cold terror seized him, a tiny moan trickling from his dry mouth. Through the large open doors, bodies were visible and they were dead, that much he could see. Sprawled out in the dust, the wind rustling through the dry, open ring of the corral, he ticked them off. Windrush, Joseph, the marshal, the stable-boy. A sudden stab of pain pierced his heart. The boy, who'd looked after him, tended his wounds. Nothing but a scrap. A child. Butchered by some lunatic. He put his head back against the stable wall and closed his eyes, trying to block it all out. But when he opened his eyes again, the truth remained. He sobbed.

Later, he managed to find water in an abandoned canteen left behind when the killers went on their way. He drank. Nothing but a mouthful, but enough for now.

The others were there, all dead. Windrush, riddled with bullets. Marshal Climes, the back of his skull gone. And Joseph. Jesus, if anything, he was the worst. He'd blown his own brains out and Francis couldn't begin to think why. Was it he who had put paid to Climes and Windrush, then turned the gun on himself, the guilt too much? Francis dismissed the notion. Why would he do such a thing? Stepping out into the open corral, averting his eyes from the lumps of bloated, rotting flesh that had once been human beings, he weaved his way across the deserted street to the saloon.

The stench hit him as he went through the batwing doors and he retched, turning away, heaving his guts out onto the boardwalk.

There were dead people everywhere.

Gathering his courage, he stepped back inside, neckerchief covering his nose and mouth, and rooted around behind what remained of the counter. He found a bottle with brown liquid inside. He took it with him as he left. The flies buzzed loudly. A hellish place.

Outside, he lifted the bottle to the sky and studied the contents. Pulling out the stopper, he took in the aroma. It might have been whisky. He took a slug, the burning liquid hitting the back of his throat like the lick of flames, and he coughed and spluttered, creasing up, holding on, the back of his hand crammed against his mouth. The pain passed and he drank again. This time, his body rode the shock, the whisky, or whatever it was, spreading its warmth through his stomach.

Sitting down on the edge of the boardwalk, he finished the bottle off and tossed it into the street. Nothing stirred, not even a stalk of dried grass. No birds winged their way across the sky. No sounds. No one.

Sighing, he stretched his legs, the alcohol doing its work. He touched one of the many lumps on his face and winced. God, he'd taken a beating, perhaps the worst he'd ever had. Windrush sure was adept at using his fists. Thing was, he wouldn't be adept at anything else ever again. The bastard was dead. Shot. Good riddance to him.

'Old Francis', they'd called him, the members of the meagre little posse who had set out from Archangel on the trail of Father Merry, the killer. Well, now all of them were killed. Including the marshal. Damn it, there would be hell to pay for that. Just who had carried out the killing, Francis didn't know. He barely recalled the raised voices and the gunshots, as he had been drifting in and out of consciousness at the time. The killers must have believed him to be already dead. He believed he have looked like it, too, after what Windrush had done to him.

He sat up and let his eyes scan the broad, open street. The buildings on the other side were empty, some boarded up. Perhaps they all were. He considered the idea of finding an old hotel, of getting some proper sleep under a blanket, with a feather pillow for his head. Fanciful perhaps, but he'd have to give it a try. He struggled to his feet and stretched out his back. He could do with a gun, too, he thought to himself. Once night-time came, this would be a fearful place to be left all alone in, with no means to defend himself.

He found a revolver close to the corral. It held four bullets. Something at least. Stuffing it into his waistband, he made his way down the street, ever watchful, senses alert for the slightest sound.

There was nothing.

He tried the doors of several buildings, all of which remained firmly locked. When he turned the corner some twenty or so paces away, a rambling hotel stood at the far end of the street, its doors wide open as if beckoning him to step inside.

Francis frowned and his fingers crept to the gun while his eyes remained firmly fixed on the entrance.

Slowly, he made his approach, certain that eyes were watching. He looked right, then left. Those other buildings, all standing so lonely and desolate, stared back at him as if mocking him. Was he heading towards danger, or just another empty and forgotten space?

Some half dozen paces from the steps leading up to the front door, Francis stopped, considering that the men who had done all the killing might be inside. He had no way of knowing how long he'd lain unconscious. The dryness of his throat attested to more than a day. The rumbling in his guts echoed the same conclusion.

Would they still be here, and for what reason? This was a dead place, a ghost town, or would very soon be one.

Even so, they might have stayed behind. Or, if not all of them, maybe a couple, waiting.

Waiting for what?

Swallowing hard, Francis drew the gun and walked on. He mounted the first step, staring at the dark interior. If there was anyone inside, surely to God they'd have shot him by now. He took the second step. Paused. Listened. The only sound was his own heartbeat, pounding in his head.

He took the third step.

The wooden stair creaked horribly, the sound, impossibly loud, breaking the unearthly silence.

Now was the time for him to die – for the bullets to come slamming into his chest as unseen assailants sent him into oblivion. He tensed. Waited.

He stepped up onto the veranda. Inscribed in the floorboards before the big, open door was the single word, *Welcome.* He had to smile at that. Taking a breath, he prepared to take a final step and cross the threshold.

And then, from behind, he heard the unmistakable sound of a horse cantering down the street and heading straight for him.

8

John Wesley sat at a table in the cantina drinking tequila neat. Positioning his chair to face the open door, he had his legs stretched out in front of him, hat tipped over his eyes, his revolver already drawn and lying on his lap.

He'd found Maria dead in the small outhouse, a single bullet-hole between her eyes – eyes which, even in death, were so beautiful. For one of the few times in his adult life, he sobbed at the sight of death… at the sight of her.

They'd come for him like they always did – cowards, in the night. He'd shot and killed two of them, but the third had somehow managed to slip round the back. It was this remaining assailant for whom he now waited, knowing he would come. They always came, to chance their luck and kill the renowned gunfighter, John Wesley Hardin.

Maria's death hit him hard. He loved her, had even entertained the notion of marrying her, settling down, perhaps even having a child. Now, all of that was gone. He already had a wife, of course. A child, too. But things had not gone well. Life did not deal the cards in his favour, despite him playing the game with all his considerable skill. In the end, the dealer would always win.

Draining the glass, he put it down and hefted the Colt in his hand, checking the load again. He twirled the cylinder and pondered pouring himself another drink. It was while shifting his gaze to the almost empty bottle that he heard it.

The tiny clink of a spur as a booted foot stepped onto the veranda.

The man came through the door, momentarily blocking out the daylight behind him. He'd made the mistake of rushing his attack. Although both his hands were filled with revolvers, it took him a second or two for his eyes to adjust to the gloom of the cantina's interior. Two seconds too long.

John Wesley put the first bullet through his jaw, the heavy caliber slug throwing him backwards to the ground.

The gunfighter waited.

The man writhed on the ground, his destroyed face a mess of blood and splintered bone. He would be dead within a few minutes. He knew it, and so did John Wesley. He deliberated over shooting the assailant again, but then decided he enjoyed seeing him suffer. Soon, the realization of the man's situation would overtake the pain, and the fear would consume him. The fear of impending death.

John Wesley casually rolled himself a cigarette, taking care not to spill any of the tobacco. A horse whinnied outside. The dying man groaned. Perhaps he wanted to say something – tell John Wesley how sorry he was, or, more likely, curse him to hell and back.

Stepping out onto the veranda, John Wesley leaned against one of a pair of posts supporting the roof and smoked. Ahead lay the open plain, a grey dustbowl hyphenated with gorse and scrub. It undulated into the distance, an unchanging vista which spoke of innumerable dangers, dried-up riverbeds, scorching sunshine, lack of shade, lack of water, lack of food. It was the direction in which he had to go if he were to escape from his many pursuers. Posses, vigilantes, bounty hunters. He had to make his way to Mexico. El Paso. There, he might be able to sink into anonymity, if only for a short time.

And try and forget Maria.

Flicking away the cigarette, he stepped down onto the ground, ignoring the dying assailant, and paused only to pick up the man's guns. They were poorly made handguns and he probably would have missed with every shot he'd fired, if he'd had the chance. Breaking them open, John Wesley shook out the bullets and flung the handguns far across the plain. Then he crossed to the horse, stroked its neck, studied its legs and flanks. She was in good condition, considering. Sheathed behind the saddle was a 'Yellow-Boy' carbine, which he took out and examined. It could do with a clean, but would prove useful. Especially when crossing the prairie… Especially if he came across marauding Comanches.

He took his time and gathered his few belongings. He had considered burying Maria, but instead asked the old taverna owner to keep her on the bed which they had shared. John Wesley had tenderly placed her arms across her chest and tucked in the bed-clothes around her. She might well be asleep if it wasn't for the bullet-hole. To disguise this, he'd carefully tied a scarf around her forehead, kissed her for the last time, and left.

Placing two more bottles of tequila in the saddlebags, he mounted his horse and led it to the front. The dying man lay sprawled on the ground, eyes wide open. They seemed to be saying something to him. The destroyed mouth a horrible, gaping hole, most of the teeth blown away, but he still managing to work what was left of the jaw up and down.

"I don't have a clue what you're trying to say, you bastard." John Wesley sent a line of spit towards him, but missed by many feet. "You should have stayed at home and kept tight hold of your mama's apron strings. Now you're dead and I hope you suffer for what you did to my Maria. Give my regards to old Lucifer when you see him. *Adios.*"

With that, he turned his horse towards the prairie and broke into a steady canter, not once turning to look back at the place where he and his only love had shared a few brief, yet precious moments together.

It was on the third day of his ride that he came upon the town. A bleak, miserable place, the buildings boarded up, nothing moving. But there were dead men in the corral and the stench of death at every turn.

Except at the hotel. For there, standing in the doorway, was a man. And in his hand, he held a gun. Reining in his horse, John Wesley drew out the 'Yellow-Boy', worked the action, and waited.

9

Santa Angelo was a 'once visited, best forgotten' kind of town. Dilapidated buildings mixed with several rundown saloons and tired whorehouses, with little else to make it into anything more than a brief stopping place. The streets were filthy, littered with rubbish, rotting food and other, unrecognizable things, mingling to create a sharp, unpleasant stench which struck the back of the throat. Dogs rummaged in the litter and in the side streets, fat rats sauntered lazily over stacks of rotting food.

But the beer and whisky ran freely.

Just the way Reece's men liked it.

They rode into the town in the late afternoon, the sun continuing to burn bright, their clothes stuck to their backs, the sweat stains large and stinking. As they dismounted outside the largest of the saloons, Reece warned them not to get into fights as they would be moving on at first light. Their destination was El Paso. "Unless we come across Merry first," he said to them.

Bobbing their heads, their attention on what waited for them beyond the batwing doors, they chuckled and went inside, their spurs pinging loud in chorus. There were four of them. Reece, still astride his horse, looked across to Willis who was busy rolling himself a cigarette. "I guess you won't be joining them?"

Shrugging, Willis tightened off his tobacco pouch with his teeth and put it inside his shirt. "Maybe I'll have a drink later. You?"

Reece shrugged. "Later. I have to find somewhere to put Toby. I don't think he's in any state to do much frolicking."

Glancing at Toby slumped across his horse's neck, Willis nodded in agreement. "I'll help you."

A little way down the street, they came across an old Mexican splayed out beneath a huge sombrero, dozing in an old rocking chair under the eaves of a closed-down mercantile store. Clearing his throat, Willis leaned forward. "Hey, *amigo*, you know anywhere we can bed down our sick friend here?"

With no answer forthcoming, Reece lost his patience and said, "Shit, Willis, he's either asleep or dead. Let's move on."

"I am neither, *señor*," said the old man, tipping back his hat. He regarded the cowboys with disgust, his mouth turned down, black, uneven teeth peeping out between cracked lips. "There is nowhere here. The only beds are those in the whorehouse, and that will cost you."

"He needs rest, is all," retorted Reece, nodding towards Toby.

The old man shrugged and leaned back, pulling his hat over his eyes. "There is nowhere."

"You bastard," spat Reece, reaching for his gun. Willis' hand came down like a clamp around his wrist. Wrenching himself free, Reece glared.

"You just told the boys not to cause trouble, boss," said Willis quickly. "Take it easy. We might find somewhere down the street. An old barn or something."

"There is nothing, you gringo sonofabitch," said the man from beneath his sombrero. "I have told you."

"We're willing to pay," said Willis. He ignored Reece's startled look.

The foreman's words had the desired effect and, as if suddenly transformed with an injection of sheer delight, the Mexican sat forward, eyes sparkling and rubbed his hands. "In that case, *señor...*" cackling, he held out a gnarled hand, "I know of a place."

Sighing, Reece shook his head, reached inside his shirt and flicked a dollar towards the old man, who caught it with surprising dexterity. He immediately put the coin between his teeth and attempted to bend the metal, to test its authenticity. Satisfied, he popped it into his shirt pocket. "I know a place. It is warm and quiet."

"Take us there," said Reece, impatience evident in his voice.

"I am old, *señor*. You, you are young. At the end of the street, take a left. Then..." He grinned. "Ah, the rest, it is not so clear in my head." He tapped his forehead with a filthy, bitten-down fingernail. "I am old, like I say."

"You bastard," snarled Reece and threw him another dollar. "And that's the last you'll get. Next piece of metal will be a bullet in your brain, what's left of it."

Chuckling, the old Mexican sat back. "Take a left, then the next right. You will come to an old livery stable. There will be a man like me. Old. Forgetful. His name is Pablo. Tell him Jaime sent you. He will want another dollar." He held up his hand to ward off any further threats. "But that is all he'll want, *señor*. The price is still better than what you'd pay in the whorehouse." And with that, he tipped the sombrero back over his face and settled into a slow, slumbering snooze.

Turning his horse away, Reece muttered, "Goddamned bastards. If he's taking us for a ride, Willis, I'll come back and—"

"No, Mr Reece, sir, I don't think it will come to that. We'll pay this Pablo his dollar and we'll all bed down for the night. The boys will find their own bunks, somehow, somewhere." He laughed. "Lucky bastards that they are."

As soon as the sound of hooves disappeared around the far corner, Jaime sprang out of his old rocking chair, ran with surprising agility across the main street and burst through the doors of the tired old cantina opposite the spot where he'd been sitting. Inside the smoke-filled confines of the tiny room, a bunch of bored-looking Mexicans huddled around a small, round table, playing cards. They all bore the telltale signs of drunkenness, their words laboured, lips slack, eyes virtually closed.

One of the men, a huge, lumbering individual, face almost totally covered by a thick, greasy beard, rounded his eyes towards Jaime and grunted. "You knock before you enter, you prairie-dog."

"Enrique," said Jaime stepping closer to the table, wringing his hands, the rim of his huge sombrero flapping like a sail caught in the breeze. "I have something for you."

Enrique spat out a scornful laugh, dismissing him with a wave of his hand. "You always have something. Problem is, it is never worth anything."

"This time is different." Emboldened, he stepped right up next to the large man. "Strangers. Three of them, one sickly. Gringos. Rich."

The others around the table sat up, interest pricked. Enrique, studying his cards, rubbed his chin. "How you know they are rich?"

"Something about the way they talked. One man called the other 'boss', and said there were 'others'. So, I'm guessing, Enrique, they are cattlemen, or ranchers."

"That is no guarantee."

"No, but their rigs are fancy, their clothes too. Especially the boss man. He is young, arrogant. A typical gringo sonofabitch. He gave me two silver dollars."

"Silver?" Enrique arched an eyebrow and Jaime nodded frantically, tongue licking his bottom lip. "You sent them to Pablo?"

"As always."

"Well, they might be worth a look." He threw down his cards. Three queens. The others groaned and Enrique laughed. "I was hoping for a full-house, but who knows, maybe after we have taken a look at these gringos…"

He pushed back his chair and stood up, adjusting the gun belt which sagged around his substantial middle. "Raul, you stay out on the porch and cover the street with the scatter gun, in case these 'others' appear. The rest of us will go and relieve these bastards of their money. We then come back and continue playing as if nothing has happened. When it is early morning, we'll go to find the others. Where are they staying, Jaime?"

"They did not say, but more than likely Arabella's."

"Yes. More than likely. Well, we'll find them, slit their throats while they sleep. If this proves profitable, Jaime, there is ten dollars in it for you."

"Only ten dollars?"

Ignoring the old man's outrage, Enrique sniggered. "It is more than your information is worth. You haven't given us anything for weeks, you coyote-loving bastard."

Everyone laughed, even the barkeep polishing glasses behind his counter. All, that is, except Jaime, who scowled and watched them all troop out. He then crossed to the bar and ordered a tequila. It was his first for over three weeks.

* * *

Pablo showed them into a dry, airy space, the smell of hay sweet in the air. Willis, supporting Toby around the waist, sighed. "My God, this smells like home."

"It does that," said Reece, pulling off his jacket. He nodded to Pablo, hovering by the door. "We'll bunk down here with our friend. There's a couple more dollars in it if you can bring us fresh coffee at sunrise."

The man, who appeared even older than Jaime, bowed from his waist, chuckling. "*Gracias, señor.*"

"It had better be fresh, though," added Reece, "or you won't get nothing but a kick up your scrawny ass."

Continuing with his low laughing, the old man disappeared into the evening air. Reece followed him to the door and looked down the street. Behind him, Willis struggled to set Toby down amongst the straw. Evening was coming on quickly. In the far distance, Reece could just pick out the sound of laughter mingling with some off-key piano playing. "Damn it if I wouldn't rather be with the boys right now."

"Why not go?" said Willis, somewhat breathlessly. "I'll stay here, make sure Mr Toby is all right. You go and get yourself a drink or two. Maybe something extra."

Reece turned. "Just a drink would be fine." His thoughts returned to Manuela. The feel of her, the smell of her perfume... How she'd stood in front of him and said that she would not be there when he got back. He squeezed his eyes shut, trying to block out the image of her face. Manuela. Those eyes... those luscious lips... those soft breasts.

"Well then, go," said Willis. He rolled Toby over onto his back. The big man groaned. "Jeez, I wonder if he'll ever regain consciousness?"

"He will. He's a stubborn bastard, hard as nails, too. I reckon after a good night's sleep, he'll be fine."

"Wonder what they was fixing on doing to him back in that flea-pit of a town where we found him? We never did get the chance to find out."

"Perhaps it's better that way. Let's hope Toby himself don't remember."

"I reckon that's true enough. So go, Mr Reece. Have a drink. Try and relax. We've got a long ride ahead of us tomorrow."

Grunting, Reece went outside. Instinctively, he checked the horses and shouted in to Willis to make sure he watered and fed them before bunking down for the night. The foreman said he would and Reece shrugged on his jacket and strolled down the street.

He did not see Pablo. Perhaps the old man had already found himself a saloon in which to spend his dollar. He didn't know and he paid the old man's absence no mind.

Until he reached the street corner and saw the others.

10

Bradley stood in the dusty sheriff's office, staring intently at several Wanted posters pinned on the notice board. He didn't hear the person creeping up behind him until a heavy hand came down on his shoulder. Startled, he jumped back, hands coming up defensively. "Sorry," he blurted.

The man standing before him was a big, barrel-chested individual whose close-set eyes regarded Bradley with a keen curiosity. He had a cruel-looking mouth and sported a wispy beard to conceal a weak chin. He wore two revolvers, handles turned inwards and a gold watch chain hung heavily above them, its fob tucked into the pocket of a patterned waistcoat. On his left jacket lapel was pinned his sheriff's star. He glowered. "Now, who in hell might you be?"

"My, er, my name is James. Bradley James. A Mister Stenton brought me here... said he knew you."

"Stenton? That crazy old coot? What the hell did he bring you to see me for?"

The office door creaked open and both looked across to see Stenton's considerable bulk filling the doorway. He pulled off his battered hat and dragged his forearm across his face. "Darn if it ain't the hottest I can recall for a long time."

The sheriff jerked his thumb backwards towards Bradley. "Who the hell is this young fella, Stenton?"

"Oh, he's just someone I picked up out on the prairie. Say, you wouldn't have any coffee, would you?" He stepped inside and the sunlight, most of which had been blocked up to that point, streamed in, causing the sheriff to raise his arm to shield himself from the glare. Stenton, taking the cue, shut the door and stomped a few paces forward. The sheriff was a powerfully-built man but Stenton towered over him.

The sheriff sighed. "No, I do not. Is he wanted?"

"No, he ain't. He wants a job, though."

"A *job*?"

"Uh-huh. Reckon you owes me one, sheriff, after what I did for you last Fall. Remember that Elmore Purdey individual who had you by the throat in the Acme? The bank robber you was meaning to arrest? I reckon you wouldn't be here right now if I hadn't stepped in."

The sheriff turned away and Bradley noticed how the man's face suddenly reddened. "Jesus, Stenton."

"Yeah, well. If I hadn't pulled him off you, he would have gutted you like a fish."

"All right," the sheriff said, a lot of his former bravado seeping away from his voice. "I'll see what I can do. They might need someone over at the livery. I'll go and ask—"

"I was thinking more likely here." Stenton grinned. "As your deputy."

The sheriff gaped. So did Bradley, who said, "Er, Mr Stenton, if I can just—"

"He'd make a fine deputy. He can shoot, he's honest and I reckon he'll do you proud. If you can see yourself willing to give him a three-month trial, I'd reckon that would make us just about even."

"Damn you," drawled the sheriff, but there was no fight left in him. He pushed his way past Stenton and strode over to a large, plain-fronted cabinet. He pulled it open, took out a bottle containing dark brown liquid, and tipped a measure into each of three glasses. He turned and offered one to Bradley and the other to Stenton. "We may as well celebrate your appointment, young fella."

Bradley shot Stenton a glance. The big man smiled and then winked. "Why not?" Bradley looked down at his glass uncertainly. Stenton downed his in one. "Hell, that tastes good."

"Three months you say?" Stenton nodded and held his hand out for a refill. The sheriff obliged. "I'm not actually legally entitled to swear him in as Deputy. I am a constable, not a sheriff, but I guess I can bend regulations a little. This is a quiet town for the most part, so things should turn out well."

"I won't let you down, sir."

The man sporting the sheriff's badge stared at the boy from beneath bristling brows. "Oh, you will. I'm sure of it. And in three months, you'll be out on your ass looking for a job in the livery, just like I offered you before."

"That won't happen, sir."

"I'll bet you a hundred dollars it will, boy." The man smiled and, before tossing his drink down his throat, drew out a bunch of crinkled bank notes. He threw them onto his desk. "I'm a man of my word. The name is John Selman. You can call me *Mister* Selman."

"Shoot, you is one arrogant sonofabitch," cackled Stenton. He shouldered Selman aside and filled up his glass again.

Bradley cleared his throat. "Up to this point, my life has been hard, but I wish to make good the time I have left to me. I fell into bad company, so perhaps the good Lord has given me the opportunity to repent by doing what's right in the service of law and order."

"By God, your words is flowery. Cut the bullshit, boy, take a firearm, then we'll go out back and you can show me how well you can shoot."

Nodding, Bradley took a sip of the drink and winced as the sharp, burning liquid hit the back of his throat. Gasping, he took a moment or two before turning back to the Wanted posters. "This individual," he tapped the nearest dog-eared poster, "you know who he is?"

Together, Selman and Stenton moved closer to study the picture. It showed a bare-headed, clean-shaven individual with dark, cold eyes. Under the face was printed, *J. W. Hardin, Alias J. H. Swain. Wanted for murder. $4,000 reward. Dead or Alive.*

"Yup," said Selman, "I know him well."

"How well, Mr Selman, sir?"

"I've had dealings with him. He shot and killed a deputy sheriff by the name of Webb over in Texas a while back. Met some girl name of Jane Bowen, who I knew well myself. They got married, ran off to Florida, even had a child from what I understand. As far as I know, there was some trouble between them and Hardin left. Went back to his home town, and there he shot Webb. He's been on the run ever since."

"Here's here."

The two older men stopped and looked at Bradley with stunned expressions. Selman recovered first. "What do you mean 'here'? In El Paso?"

"No. Close by. I came across him. It was him that left me in the desert to die."

"That's how I found him," said Stenton quickly. "Some red-skinned savage was trying to kill him. I saved him."

Bradley felt the heat rising from under his collar. To hide his discomfort, he swung around to face the poster. "He saved my life, then left me for dead."

"Why would he do that?"

"Because he took exception to what I told him about a coloured man I once knew. Seems this Hardin don't like coloured folk. When I tried to explain my reasons, he got as wild as a penned-up racoon and left me without a horse or water. Bastard was laughing when he rode off."

"He is an uncaring piece of dog shit, that's for sure," said Selman. He put his hand on Bradley's shoulder, but this time with a good deal more thoughtfulness. Bradley turned and looked at him. He smiled. "Thank God for old Stenton here, eh?"

"Yes. Thank God." He pulled in a deep breath. "I won't let you down, Mr Selman, I promise you. For now I have a reason, a very good reason, not to. I'm going to practise my shooting every day, and I'll carry out all my duties with due regard to law and order. You teach me and I'll learn. I give you my word."

"Well hell, boy, I could ask for nothing more."

"I have only one request."

Selman stiffened slightly, the frown deepening in his dark face. "And what might that be?"

"When we meet up with this Hardin, you leave me alone with him for five minutes." And then he smiled. By the look on the faces of other two, it was a smile which sent a chill through their hearts.

After Bradley had demonstrated his prowess with both rifle and handgun, Selman, openly impressed, clapped him on the shoulder and welcomed him to the service of the law. Stenton accompanied the young man to the livery stable, where they were to stay until Bradley found more permanent lodgings.

"I'm going to get myself a drink," said the big Indian-fighter. "Selman's bourbon has given me a taste."

Sitting on a stack of hay bales, Bradley studied his newly acquired revolver. "What you said, about that Indian trying to kill me."

"Ah yeah, *him.* I ain't ever seen anything like that. Damned if I ain't."

"His name was Man Alone. He saved my life."

Stenton frowned. "Well, shit… it didn't look to me as if he was saving anyone." Grunting, he turned around and swayed out of the door.

Reports were vague, as there were no witnesses to what happened, save for those who said Stenton left the saloon sometime after midnight, considerably drunk.

His dead body was found down a side alley. He'd been stabbed from behind in what the doctor called a 'frenzied attack'. When Selman woke Bradley in the morning to tell him what happened, the young man sat and shook his head. "Damn," was all he said.

But when Selman left, Bradley smiled and gently patted the heavy-bladed hunting knife sheathed at his hip.

11

"I'm not sure if he's going to make it."

Nati was sitting in the back of the wagon, pressing a damp cloth against Father Merry's feverish forehead every few seconds. Twisting himself around to study the two of them, Ritter pulled a face. "We're less than a day away now. We should make it before sundown."

"What if we don't?"

Ritter could only offer a resigned look. "I can't go any faster. The trail is so rutted, it would probably kill him."

"Do you even know where we're going?"

A shrug. What else could he give? This land was unknown to him and, using Merry's vague directions, he'd set a course which he hoped was roughly south-west. The trail was old, probably hadn't been used for decades, and nothing about the surrounding landscape gave him any clues. Only his very basic knowledge of how the sun appeared in the sky helped him, but he was well aware of how his ignorance in such matters could so easily lead them astray. Remaining on the trail was the best he could do. Distances, however, were nothing more than wild guesses.

"Listen, why don't I scout ahead, make for higher ground and try and get a better idea that way?"

She thought for a moment. Merry lay quiet, his breathing even. He'd lost a lot of blood but he was a big man; strong, too. She nodded. "All right. But don't be long, Gus."

"I won't."

After he'd untied his horse from the rear of the wagon, he spurred it along the trail and had soon left the trundling wagon far behind. He headed off to the west, gaining the high ground with little difficulty. The hills closest to the trail were low and, with not much in the way of rocky outcrops and thorny scrub to hold him up, the horse could pick its way without much hindrance. Soon, the trail was far below, the wagon appearing like a child's toy.

He made the rise and peered out across the sprawling plain.

Way to the east, the silver thread of a river wound its way through the uniform grey of the land. Edged with green, occasional clumps of trees brought the promise of fresh water and shade from the relentless sun. But it was far away, perhaps too far.

Squinting in the dazzling light, he thought he saw a vague smudge of brown on the horizon. It might be buildings, but just as easily it could be simple differences in the shape and colour of the land. He dropped down from the horse, shaded his eyes from the sun's glare and tried to make some sense of what it might be.

It could be buildings. A town. Especially as the trail headed unerringly towards it. If this was indeed the place Merry had told them about, it was approximately a day's wagon-ride away. Alone, on his horse, he could make it in half that time. But what would be the use in that, he wondered. He dropped his hand and stood, trying his best to calculate the distance. The heat-haze didn't help and he reminded himself that out here, in this featureless expanse, the eyes could so easily be tricked.

A movement caught his attention. He narrowed his eyes. Shapes, closer this time, much more discernible. He instantly dropped to his stomach and wriggled forward on his belly to the edge of the escarpment and focused in on what he'd seen.

A camp. Small, but obvious. A trickle of smoke and two men. No. He looked again. Three men. And a smaller one. A child. A single pony. They were too far away for Ritter to see much more, but the pony might mean Indians. Too few for a war-party, they might be hunters, but hunting for what? There was no game out here, at least nothing worth bothering with. Perhaps they were heading for the river, where the woodland might hold deer, certainly rabbits. The thought of rabbit brought the flavour to his mouth and he drooled, stomach rumbling. But, as he'd already noted, the river was far off. Much farther than the town, if the brown smudge was a town.

Three Indians and a boy.

It was curious that they should be so exposed, so far from anything.

A sudden flash of movement snapped his attention back to the tiny group. The boy was running, head down, as fast as his small legs could carry him. He heard the whoops of the others, saw one of them jump onto the back of the pony, running the boy down within a few blinks. Indians, definitely. Scooping him up, the rider turned about and headed back to his companions at a steady trot. He threw the boy down to the ground. Ritter could clearly see it was a boy. Short-haired, blue serge trousers – store-bought, possibly. A farmer's boy. A white boy.

One of the others back-handed him to the ground and the boy remained sprawled in the dirt whilst the others took to breaking up their camp.

He could be upon them within the hour.

Chewing his bottom lip, he thought of Nati… of how she might feel if he didn't return. *Don't be long.* Hesitating, he wrestled with indecision. She'd be out of her mind with worry. She'd rein in the wagon and go searching for him, leaving Merry behind, every second so vital to his survival. The priest would be dead by the end of the day. They had to make the town and if that smudge was it, then they had every chance of saving the padre's life. A doctor, a warm bed, care.

Then again, if those Indians had kidnapped the boy, what would their intentions be?

Could he leave a child to their excesses and their cruelty?

He made his decision, checked his Colt and slithered back to his horse. Using the ridge as his cover, he led the animal across to his left, keeping out of sight of those in the searing basin far below. When he felt it was safe to do so, he mounted up and rode off in a wide arc, mindful of how adept Indians were at picking up the sound of approaching horses. He'd swing well away from them before turning, dismounting, and easing his way behind them. With any luck, he'd be upon them before they knew what was happening.

With any luck.

They were tired, hungry and ill-tempered. Already, they had quarrelled over the wisdom of bringing the boy who, even now, sat upright, his eyes glaring out his hatred. He'd tried more than once to escape and would no doubt try again, no matter how many times they beat him. He was sullen, and neither spoke nor begged for food, which was just as well as there wasn't any. Every stomach convulsed in agony.

The river gave them some hope. If not game, then fish – anything to fill their bellies and take away the horrible wrenching and constant pain from which they all suffered.

"My name is Jeremiah," he'd told them, once they knew no one was following them. "And I'll see you all in hell, by God."

"God?" said one of them, the eldest, flecks of grey in his blue-black hair, hanging down in greasy threads to his thin shoulders. "Your god will not help you. No one will."

He'd translated for the others and they'd laughed.

That was several afternoons ago.

No one had laughed since.

Now, his lip throbbing, Jeremiah tenderly probed the place where the Indian had struck him. He tasted blood and now, looking at the back of his hand, the small dab of red confirmed it. The eldest Comanche hit him several times a day. The worst had been when he'd made his first attempt to escape. He remembered the fists, the kick in the groin and he winced, slumping so that his head hung down between his knees. Damn them, he'd kill them if he got the chance. But how could that chance ever come? There were three of them, and Ma and that heathen Chinaman, who'd tried so hard to save them, were long gone. Dear God, they might even be dead.

Grandpa was dead. Nasty old Grandpa. He'd never been shy when it came to meting out punishment, but he'd almost always preferred the belt. He'd say it was God's work he was doing, that the devil had to be beaten out, "Else you'll go astray, boy". He'd hated Grandpa for the way he used that damned belt, and he'd hated Ma for sitting idly by and letting it happen. Ma never was right in the head. She would break down in tears every night, ranting against everyone and everything. She enjoyed seeing Jeremiah get his beatings and she'd often laugh.

Pa never would have let such things happen. But Pa was dead, too, shot by some miserable coward over in town. Ma had spoken his name once, but Jeremiah could not recall it – especially not now, with his mind so full of other things – the hopelessness of his situation, the horror of being taken by these godless savages. He was the last of his family and he was going to end his days with these redskins. He groaned and broke down, the strength draining out of him as freely as the tears which rolled down his face and dripped into the dust.

Then the shooting started.

He didn't know the direction, nor did he care. Snapping his head up, he stared around him wildly. The three savages were on their feet. One of them had a rifle and it was he who received the first two bullets. They smacked into him with the force of a charging buffalo, flinging him backwards off his feet. He hit the ground hard, the rifle clattering from his already dead fingers.

Jeremiah didn't think.

There was no time to think.

He dashed to the gun. But so did the eldest savage. For a fleeting moment, their eyes met and Jeremiah saw the man's fear. Perversely, this gave him a surge of hope and strength, and he sprang forward. The Indian was there, too, stooping down to seize the rifle, so Jeremiah put his boot into the man's face, kicking him as hard as he could. The Indian yelped and fell to the side. There was more gunfire, but Jeremiah didn't care about that. All his attention was on the rifle. His hands closed around it and he turned.

The Indian was in a half-crouch, knife in one hand, tomahawk in the other.

He was grinning.

Jeremiah worked the lever and fired.

For a moment, it was as if the entire world was mocking him. Laughing. Grandpa had always said God had a sense of humour. He never mentioned how sick that sense of humour was.

The gun was empty.

Ritter walked forward at an even pace. He put two bullets into the one with the rifle first. The others had close-fighting weapons, so he discounted them for the moment. He saw the boy scampering towards the dead Indian, and he also spotted an older warrior with grey hair rushing to take up the fallen rifle. The third warrior took his attention now, coming at him fast and low, screaming his war-cry. Ritter waited calmly, dispassionately and, when he was no more than two paces away, he emptied his revolver into the redskin, sending him into a wild, convulsing dance of death.

He worked quickly now, feeding in fresh cartridges, one eye on the others. He saw the boy kicking the warrior, picking up the rifle, firing.

No sound. No bullets.

The Comanche gave a whoop of victory and readied himself to spring forward.

He was ten, maybe twelve paces away.

Ritter put a bullet into the back of his head. The subsequent silence was almost as frightening as the brief, deadly skirmish had been.

Recovering, the boy turned his wide eyes towards Ritter who, holstering his gun, walked slowly forward, offering a friendly smile, raising his right hand, his gun hand, to show there was no threat, no danger. "It's all right, son," he said.

But he could see in the boy's anguished expression that he was far from all right. Dropping to his knees, he went into a kind of fit. White spittle frothed from his mouth and his entire body went into spasm, legs stuck out rigid, eyes rolling into the back of his skull.

Quickly, Ritter ran to him, held him in his arms and watched, with growing horror, how the boy's teeth sank ever more deeply into his lower lip. The blood bubbled up to mix with the saliva, turning it a ghastly shade of pink. Ritter didn't know what to do, so he held onto the boy, held him tight, doing his best to comfort him with words of reassurance. He didn't know if the boy could hear anything, but then, just as quickly as it had begun, the fit subsided. The boy's body grew limp and heavy, breathing growing deep and more regular.

Even so, Ritter continued to hold him. And when the boy's eyes finally flickered open, Ritter smiled. Remarkably, so did the boy.

12

Pushing through the kitchen door with his shoulder, Francis walked into the hotel lobby with two plates piled high with eggs and slices of ham. He put them down at the table chosen by Hardin and mumbled, "The bread was covered in green mould, but the rest, which I found in a cold store, seems fine."

"Taste will tell," said the gunfighter, and attacked the food without another word.

Eating at a more leisurely pace, Francis paused to pour out beer from a pitcher. "There is plenty of this," he said, raising his glass.

Grunting with his mouth full, Hardin nodded and tapped his glass with his knife. He continued to eat whilst Francis poured the beer.

Having finished, Hardin positioned his chair by the open door and gazed down the street. After studying him for a few silent moments, Francis decided to draw up his own chair and sat down beside him.

"Wonder why everyone left?"

Hardin shrugged, sipped his beer and stretched out his legs. His eyes never left the street. "It happens. I've travelled through any number of ghost towns, some abandoned a long time ago, others just recently. I went through such a place where one lonely old man was the only inhabitant. He said it had been that way for over ten years. When I asked him how he survived, he told me Indians wandered through every now and then and dropped off supplies. They treated him like some sort of lucky charm, or magical portent. That was what *he* said, anyways. Me, I just think they saw him as a crazy old coot, and Indians hate crazies. Makes 'em jittery, so they treat 'em kindly, not wishing to offend spirits and the like."

"I've never had much dealings with Indians. I used to track for the army, and the fella I rode with was a Kiowa. Nice enough fella, but awful quiet. Never heard him say much more than two words at a time."

"You tracked for the army?"

"Way back. Before the War between the states." He grinned. "I'm older than I look."

"Darn it, you must be as old as the hills."

Chuckling, Francis took a swig of beer. "You could say that, yessir, you could."

"You ever shoot anyone?"

"Hell no, thank God. Saw a lot of killin', but none of it by my hand."

"Well, you're blessed if that is the case. Killing and me, we is best friends. Always have been. What you doing here, anyway?"

"I was part of a posse out of Archangel. Thought it would be a three-day thing – track down the perpetrator, bring him to justice. Then we bumped into the Scrimshaw bunch and that was when the trouble started." He eyed Hardin cautiously, hoping his twisted truth would not be too evident. But Hardin appeared disinterested, keeping most of his concentration on the street. "Can I ask… who is it you're waiting for?"

"Oh, just about anyone. I have a lot of folk on my trail." For the first time, he regarded Francis for more than a couple of seconds. "I am wanted across three, maybe four states. Not for anything I'd call sinful, mind you. I have been wrongfully accused, but the truth don't hold much water for them as wants me in the ground."

Francis shifted uneasily in his chair. He'd already noticed the guns at the man's waist, and now found himself studying them with a much keener interest. "Did you kill someone?"

Hardin's eyes turned again to the street. "A cheating, back-biting scoundrel was what he was. He'd been sworn in as a deputy, although God alone knows how. He had a grudge against me for some past indiscretion. It often happens. I tend to fall into bad circumstances, almost always not of my own making. Anyways, this bastard decides he's going to kill me, but I got the drop on him, shot him stone dead. Trouble is, him being a lawman and all, I had to high-tail it out of there as quick as I could.

"I was trying to make my way home. My first wife, she'd taken ill and died over in Florida so I had it in my mind to start again, so to speak. Anyways, that was all put to bed by what happened. Made it through Texas and across to New

Mexico. Worked on a cattle trail for a while. Darned if I didn't get myself into another brush, trying to help some young fella out. I failed and he got himself shot in the cross-fire. Damn it all if he didn't have a fiancée. I felt bad about that. But those bastards who were trying to kill him, I put them away for good, sent them to hell. But a posse was called and I found myself fleeing for my life again. So you see, even when all I want to do is help some poor unfortunate, I gets caught up in all the shit and all the misunderstanding."

"Couldn't you have stayed, tried to explain what had happened?"

"Hell, they'd string me up before I'd gotten out a single word!" He laughed, finished his beer and settled the glass on the floor next to him. "No, getting the hell away is always the best option for me. But bad luck is my constant companion. I went to visit an old flame of mine. A beautiful girl. Should have married her years ago. Well, damned bounty hunters made a play and she got killed." He shook his head and grew quiet. Francis decided to do the same.

Throughout the day, Hardin hovered by the door, rarely moving more than a few paces from it. Occasionally, he'd take one of his revolvers and check the load, sometimes replacing cartridges with others he had in his belt and vest pockets. Often a mistiness would drift over his eyes, as if he were looking back, or possibly even forwards, to what his life held or might hold.

Francis would bring him coffee and bourbon from the well-stocked bar. "If we could live on whisky, we could stay here forever," he said, counting off the bottles behind the large counter, arranged like smartly trained soldiers standing at attention.

But Hardin didn't reply. Instead, he leaned in the doorway with the nearest batwing door pulled open, and he'd stay like that for long moments, watchful, pensive.

Sometime close to evening, with the sun settling behind the distant mountains in the west, he took in a deep, resigned breath. "I been thinking about what you said."

Pricking up his ears, Francis stepped up to him. "Oh? Which part?"

"About how I should have stayed and explained that business with Webb." He gave Francis a look. "The deputy I shot."

"Ah. Well, there ain't much you can do about any of that now. Perhaps if you—"

"No. You see, that's just it. I think I can."

"I don't get you."

"Since Maria …" He grew wistful again, and turned his moist eyes back to the street. "Thing is, after the death of my wife, I had decided to leave my life of trouble behind me. I took to thinking more and more of Maria. I thought to settle down with her. Even though she, too, has gone now, I still want to settle down and I reckon there is only one way to do it. This life of always watching my back…" He shook his head. "I can't do it no more."

"So… what are you thinking of doing?" Francis wanted to ask, 'One more gunfight?' but decided that was perhaps a question too far. He waited.

"I'm going to go back, hand myself over to the law." He turned to Francis and smiled. "I shall defend myself in court, tell them the God's honest truth, and take their punishment as the judge deems fit."

"But they might hang you."

"Yes, they might. But if God is indeed merciful, then I will escape the noose and perhaps receive a light sentence. Maybe only ten years or so if I can get my conviction reduced to manslaughter. I'll plead mitigating circumstances." He winked. "I am something of a student of the law. I will defend myself well."

With that, he stepped away from the door and, for the first time since they met, he appeared relaxed, as if an inner conflict he'd been battling with all this time had at last come to its conclusion. One he could live with. He smiled, patted Francis on the shoulder and moved towards the broad, winding staircase at the rear of the hotel lobby. "I'm going to sleep in one of them fancy beds. In the morning, I'll be gone."

Francis, taking up the vigil at the door, watched the man disappear upstairs. Something told him he would never lay eyes on him again.

13

Reece burst through the barn doors at a run, throwing the Sharps rifle towards Willis while he checked his own Winchester.

"What in tarnation is going on, boss?"

"Bumped into a group of mean-looking gentlemen packing irons. I turned and ran back and they took a shot or two at me. Seems like we have been trussed up ready for the pot by that mealy-mouthed Mexican. He took us for being rich and stupid."

"Stupid we aint," said Willis and shuffled over to the doors. Stooping down on one knee, he peered through the crack into the gloom of the night. "What's the plan?"

"Shoot the bastards as they come round the corner. I reckon once we take out the head honcho, the others will scoot."

"And if they don't?"

"Then we shoot them, too."

"Nothing like half measures, Mr Reece."

"I ain't ever been a man to run from a fight. As those sonsofbitches are about to discover."

Chuckling, Willis checked his load and put his eye back to the crack.

They waited.

Laughing, Enrique replaced the two spent cartridges into his still smoking Colt and turned a jaundiced eye towards his closest companion. "Angel, you and Roberto go around the back." He jutted his chin to the buildings on the other side of the street. "Take one of those oil lamps from outside the stores. When we start shooting, you put the burning lamp against the rear wall. It will smoke them out."

"You reckon they will fight good, boss?"

A broad smile spread across Enrique's face. "Jaime was right – they are rich ranchers. You saw the chaps and the spurs that the one who ran wore. They will know how to shoot. Paco, you and me, we keep them busy but we keep our heads down. They will have rifles."

Paco brandished his own. "Me, too."

"*Si*, but they are not drunk!"

Laughing loudly, they spread out to carry out Enrique's orders.

Somewhere close by, a cockerel made its presence known. Paco winced. "That's a bad omen," he muttered, trembling hands loading up his Winchester.

"Like I said – *you* are drunk." Chuckling, he moved off at a half-crouch towards the street corner.

"I don't see anything," said Willis, from his position at the door.

"They'll come." Reece stepped over to Toby and gave him a kick in the ankle. His half-brother grunted, dashed away an imaginary blow with his hand and rolled over onto his side. Reece dropped to his knees and shook Toby hard by the shoulder. His groans grew louder.

"I think I see someone," said Willis from the door.

Ignoring him, Reece shook Toby again. "Let me be, you bastard," he moaned.

"Toby, you brain-dead idiot, you need to wake up." He shook him again.

"I am awake, damn your hide." Toby sat up, clamping palms into his eyes. After a few moments of fearful rubbing, he dropped them and looked around. "Where in hell am I?"

"Up to your neck in manure, as usual."

"Reece?" Toby squinted through the gloom. The only light available was from a solitary oil lamp which gave off a dreadful, rancid smell.

"Well, who the hell else, you halfwit?"

"Jesus, I thought you was dead!" Whooping out a cry of joy, he threw his arms around his half-brother and hugged him close. He blubbed, tears cascading down his face, soaking Reece's shirt front in an instant. "Oh, dear God, Reecey-boy, I didn't think I'd ever see you again."

Unable to detach himself, Reece twisted his head towards Willis. "Anything?"

"Just a movement. Might be a shadow, or moonlight. I'm not sure."

"Just shoot it."

"Shoot what?" Sniffing loudly, Toby pushed himself away. "What are we doing here?"

"Don't you remember anything?"

"I remember some old guys trying to stove-in my head. I shot them, then stepped outside to find two of the weirdest looking critters I ever did see pointing rifles right at me."

"Critters? You mean animals?"

"They sure weren't from this world, Reecey-boy. Anyways, they took me off to a huge house and I saw hooks in the ceiling and ropes on the ground. That's when one of 'em hit me. Hit me real hard. From that point on, I don't remember diddly."

"I think it's a person."

Reece snapped his head around. "Then shoot him, for Christ's sake!"

"Shoot who?" bawled Toby, feeling for his own gun which wasn't there. "What the fuck is going on?"

"Damn it all, Willis, shoot the bastard!"

"I might miss."

"Miss or not, just shoot him!"

Willis finally did as instructed.

The subsequent gunshot sounded like an enormous clap of thunder in the thick, stuffy confines of the stable. Toby screeched, clamping his hands to his ears and Reece instinctively ducked low.

The responding gunfire was rapid and concentrated. Red-hot pieces of lead ripped through the flimsy wooden planks of the barn, splintering the wood in a shower of jagged pieces. Struck in the face and neck, Willis staggered back. "Bastards have gotten round the sides."

"I told you to shoot whatever it was," said Reece, handing Toby his handgun. "We're in a mess, no doubt about it, Toby. You shoot whoever comes through those doors."

Another fusillade of gunfire exploded through the now virtually useless doors and Willis pitched backwards, throwing up his arms, a deep grunt escaping from deep within him. He lay amongst the straw and did not move.

"Ah, shit," spat Reece and put several blind shots through the door.

And then the rear wall erupted in an orange glow, which crept along the bottom edge in both directions with frightening speed. Black, acrid smoke quickly followed, the barn's ancient timbers being tinder dry.

"To hell with this!" roared Toby, climbing to his feet. "Damned if I'm gonna burn to death in here!" he raged above the sound of burning wood, as the flames gathered force behind him. He scrambled over to Willis and drew the man's revolver. With a gun in each hand and smoke swirling around his feet as the straw and hay ignited, he kicked his way through the shattered barn doors and ran out into the night.

Teeth clamped, Reece squinted after him, the smoke causing him to cough and retch. Keeping low, he stepped out into the night and what he believed was certain death.

"What in the hell is that?"

They all stopped, wide-eyed, listening intently. The noise in the busy saloon faded to a dull murmur as everyone's attention was drawn to the sound of gunfire.

"Hell, if that ain't Reece and Mr Toby."

"You don't know that, Coop."

Coop stood up, cards forgotten. But not his bourbon. He threw it down his throat in one swallow, smacked his lips and drew his gun. "I ain't waiting to find out, Pete." He nodded to his other companions. "Let's go and see what all the fuss is about."

Raul, positioned where Enrique told him to wait, rubbed his eyes and yawned. He longed for another tequila, then his bed. In hindsight, he wished he'd brought the bottle with him, to sustain him during this sentry duty. Smacking his lips, he considered returning to the cantina. The more he tried not to think about it, the more the lure of a triple measure of his one true love grew larger in his mind. And his mouth. Who would know? Those idiot gringos would be splayed out on the whorehouse floor by now, with Arabella going through their pockets, so no harm done. No harm at all. Rolling his shoulders, he hobbled back inside.

The little room was almost empty now, except for Jaime and Pablo sitting in the corner, quietly drinking Enrique's reward money. They barely raised their eyes when Raul marched over to the counter and demanded a drink. It took only a moment, but as soon as the little glass was brim-full, he picked it up and drank as if it were his first for weeks. Sighing, allowing the alcohol to travel with delicious heat down into the very depths of his guts, he clung onto the bar, head down. "Damn. I needed that."

Something caught the barman's eye and he nudged Raul in the shoulder. "You better go check that out," he said.

Frowning, Raul turned drunkenly and saw a figure, nothing more than a blur, sprinting across the open doorway. "What the...?" He went to scoop up the scatter gun, then remembered he'd left it outside. "Oh, *madre de Dios,*" he said and teetered across the room and peered outside.

He saw three figures disappearing into the night. Cursing, he went to draw the revolver at his hip when a voice cut through the night. "I wouldn't do that if I were you."

Turning slowly, he found himself staring into the twin barrels of his own scatter gun. He groaned.

"How many are you?"

"Eh?"

"Trying to kill my friends. How many?"

"Eh, *señor, por favor,* I know nothing of what you say."

The man eased back the twin hammers. "Take a wild guess."

Without hesitation, Raul spluttered, "Four, *señor.* But please, you must—"

Both barrels discharged, sending Raul flying backwards, his chest a latticework of blood and shredded clothing. He writhed in the dirt. Coop went across and relieved him of his gun. He looked around to see two wizened old Mexicans swaying in the doorway. He stood up and shot them both. When the bartender came flying to their aid, he shot him, too. This wasn't the time to be asking any questions.

He then set off after his friends.

Enrique screamed as the black demon erupted from out of the blazing barn. He could not make out its features, but it was huge, its hair wild. "Kill it!" Enrique yelled and Paco, standing beside him, worked his rifle, cursing with every shot fired.

But the demon kept coming, dismissive of the bullets whizzing around him, dismissive of the danger, dismissive of the threat of death. It was indestructible, whatever hellish fiend it was.

Surrendering to the terror wringing his insides so tight, he thought every fibre might snap, Enrique turned on his heels and ran.

He kept running until the three men spread out across the street opened up their guns on him in a single volley.

"Oh, Jesus," breathed Paco, his rifle empty. He threw it down and stood up, revolver in hand. The demon stepped closer.

No demon, then. A man. Huge, lumbering, grinning like someone insane. Perhaps he was. Paco didn't dare ask. He didn't get the chance.

The two guns came up and fired.

Reece fell onto the ground, coughing his guts up into the dry, dusty earth. He lay there, throat thick with smoke, tongue coated with the awful taste of ash and soot. Blinded by his watering eyes, he tried his best to raise himself up, but collapsed back down again, gasping with the effort. A horrible yawning sound swallowed up everything else and he rolled over onto his back, desperately bringing up his Winchester.

But the Winchester was of no use to him as the crumbling, fire-consumed barn gave up its efforts to stay erect and came crashing down all around him in a massive, deafening crash of smouldering, burning timber.

"*Reece!*" screamed Toby and raced towards his stricken brother, writhing in the flames. But even as he ran, Toby knew he was already too late.

14

Kicking the dust from his boots, Connick stepped through the door of the sheriff's office and doffed his hat at the man scowling at him from behind his desk.

"Evening, Sheriff. I am Lieutenant Connick of the United States Cavalry. I wonder if I may impose myself upon your good self for a moment?"

Clearly unimpressed, the lawman's reply was to produce a cigar from the inside of his frock coat. He bit off the end and spat it into the corner, then clamped the cigar between his teeth. "Say your piece fast, I'm about to close up for the day."

"Then luck, or fate, or whatever you wish to call it, is certainly with me this day."

"I don't believe in such things. Things are what they are. Nothing more. What in hell do you want?" He fumbled in his desk drawer and produced a long match, then struck it along the underneath of the desk and put the flame to his cigar. He puffed at it and waited.

"I have a prisoner. I'm escorting him to Fort James, but clearly won't make it by nightfall. Comanches are abroad, Sheriff. We don't want to get caught in a firefight with them during nighttime."

"Ah, shoot. You want to hold him here 'til morning?"

"That would be my wish, yes, sir."

"It'll cost you."

Connick blinked, momentarily taken off-balance. "I beg your pardon?"

"Fifty dollars."

"Sheriff, I am a servant of the United States Government and have no permissions to—"

"Price just went up to a hundred. You either pay it, or you find somewhere else to bunk him down. Dangerous, is he?"

"Extremely."

"One hundred and fifty." He stood up, blowing out a stream of smoke. "And if he wants breakfast, it'll be a round two hundred. What do you say?"

"I say you are a scoundrel, Sheriff, and I shall report you as soon as I reach Fort James."

"Well now, I'm all a-jitter with that there threat. I've a mind to call it two hundred without the breakfast."

"And I've a mind to seize this jailhouse in the name of the Government! I have a dozen troopers outside to enforce it if need be."

"Lieutenant, this is Prairie Rise, one of the roughest, meanest towns this side of the Pesos. It has been my life's work controlling it and nobody so much as spits without my say-so. Putting it bluntly, I have an entire *town* here that will force you and your damned troopers out of its limits if I tell 'em to. So get off your damned high-horse and give me my fucking money."

Within ten minutes, Han stood behind the closed and locked jail door and looked out across the room to see Connick counting out a pile of dollar bills. The sheriff appeared pleased and handed the keys across to the lieutenant. "Make sure you lock up," he said, patted Connick on the shoulder and went out, folding the bills into a thick wad as he did so.

Blowing out a long breath, Connick glanced across at the Okinawan. "I don't know what it is you have done, but you better be worth the trouble, that's all I can say."

Without answering, Han slumped down on the narrow bed which ran along one side of the cramped jailhouse. There was no blanket.

Connick opened the door and shouted out, "Trooper Wade, you will take first watch over the prisoner. Scarrow, you'll take second watch." He looked back at Han. "Don't you cause me no trouble, you hear? I've had a bellyful of that already."

A tall, rangy cavalry trooper eased past his commanding officer, saluting briefly as he did so. He glared at Han and took up a position close to the desk. "I'm mighty hungry, Lieutenant."

"I'll get someone to rustle up something. We'll requisition a barn for the night. Don't fall asleep, Wade."

"I won't, sir."

Connick grunted and went outside.

No sooner had the door closed than Wade crossed to the jail's iron bars and gripped them with both hands. His face contorted into that of a wild man. "You Chinese bastard, I've lost a good night's sleep because of you. One peep and I'll shoot you dead, you hear me?" He rattled the bars for effect, then stormed back to the desk and flopped down on the chair. He threw his long legs over the desk, leaned back and tipped his hat over his eyes.

Almost at once, the door creaked open and Susannah came in. Wade sat bolt upright, his eyes feasting on her body. Ignoring him, she went directly to the jail. She was smiling as she spoke, "They'll hang you, you know."

Sitting with his clasped hands between his knees, Han barely moved. "No doubt they will."

"I'll be taking myself a front seat to watch you die, you heathen bastard."

Shaking his head, Han swung around and curled himself up on the bench. Susannah stood and watched him for a moment, then swung around to find the young soldier looking at her, bewilderment in his eyes. "He as good as killed my boy's grandpa and let those red bastards who attacked us take my boy, too. It's all his fault."

"I see... Well, ma'am, in the morning, the Lieutenant will be escorting him to Fort James. He'll face trial there, so your testimony will be crucial."

"I don't see why we just don't kill him now. This is a rough old town where people get shot every day. I should know – it happened here to my own husband."

Wade blew out a breath. "If it were up to me, ma'am, I'd sooner see him dead than waste my sleeping time watching over him – but orders is orders, ma'am. I'd be put on a charge if anything happened to him."

Grunting, she went outside without another word.

"She sure is mad," muttered Wade and went back to sitting with his feet on the table.

Inside the jail, the tears slowly trickled down Han's cheeks. To have come so far in his search for his sister and to have ended up here. For all he knew, she may well be at the end of the street in some saloon or other right at this very moment. Fate, and this God-awful country, had brought him nothing but despair. Even so, as he tried his best to sleep, he mumbled an old, forgotten prayer to the spirits of his ancestors, pleading for some form of intervention, some unlooked-for chance to turn everything around. Never, in all his life, had he ever asked for anything. But now was different. Desperation and hopeless-ness had brought him to this juncture. There was simply nothing else left for him to do.

15

They laid Reece on an old piece of tarpaulin one of the cowhands had found and, with one at each corner, they carried him down the street, with Toby covering them all the while with his revolvers cocked and ready.

At Arabella's, they eased Reece onto the floor. His moans were low and continuous. Around them, stunned faces gaped, not truly understanding what had happened.

"Oh, sweet Jesus," said a middle-aged, ample-sized woman, make-up applied in thick layers on a face desperate for sunlight. She turned away, hand to her mouth, gagging. Someone else in a far corner could not hold their own vomit in. They were not alone.

Reece lay rigid and black, his body charred to a crisp in places. His hands and arms were like twisted twigs of charcoal and the flesh on his face and throat was burned off, exposing seeping red under-layers. His lips and nose no longer existed and his eyes, huge orbs of brilliant white, looked out from a head singed raw. Smoke seeped from his nostrils and ears. He was alive with agony.

In the stark light of the whorehouse, the cowhands saw the extent of his injuries for the first time. All of them wept. Toby, standing over his brother, stared at his mutilated body, mute with shock and disbelief. How could anyone live through this?

"We have to find a doctor," he mumbled.

"There ain't one here," said Arabella, at last finding the strength and the courage to look at the stricken thing on the floor once more. "Nearest doc is in the next town."

Turning his eyes to the painted lady, he swallowed hard before finding his voice. "That can't be. You must have someone here."

She shook her head, slowly coming out of her dazed state. She clapped her hands hard. Her many customers snapped their faces towards her. "We're closing up, people. Make your way home and we'll see you tomorrow."

"Ah shit, Arabella," came a voice from somewhere, "I just laid down some good money for a—"

"Everything is on the house tomorrow evening, but for now, just get the hell out!"

Without further ado, they did as they were bid, some of the whores escorting disappointed customers to the entrance, planting silent kisses on grizzled cheeks. There were a few angry murmurs, but no one argued, as most of them were almost certainly thankful to escape the horror of what lay in the centre of the room.

When it was quiet, Arabella poured out drinks for Toby and his men. They drank in silence.

Clearing his throat, Toby moved up next to her at the bar. "How far is this town?"

"Less than three hours, but you'll need to take it slow. I have a covered wagon you can use."

"You're mighty kind, lady. Thank you."

"It's the least I can do for him. Hell, I ain't ever seen anything like that. Who is he?"

"My brother."

Her face went ashen and, with her lower lip quivering, she rested her hands on his. "Oh, dear God, I'm so sorry. How in hell did it happen?"

"We was attacked by some Mexican bastards out to take our money. But myself and my men here, we put them in the ground, every last one."

"Enrique, that would be. He's done for quite a few tenderfoots over the years."

"He won't be doing it to no more." He finished his drink. "We'll leave straight away, if that's all right with you, ma'am."

She tilted her head. "You come back quick, you hear?" Toby frowned. "You're an interesting man. Big, too. I like my men big."

"I bet you do."

A giggle. She brushed her fingers along his arm. "I hope everything works out for your brother. The doc over there is a man called Wainright. He's a good man. He serves the railroad workers damned well, so I hear. There are a great many accidents, some," she looked across at Reece, groaning on the floor, "from burns and the like. He'll know what to do."

"Thank you kindly." He smiled and squeezed her hand. "I *will* come back, as soon as he's fixed up. I hope it's sooner rather than later."

In response, she gave him her own smile. "Let's hope it's sooner. But take your time. I ain't going anywhere."

Toby nodded and turned to the others. "Boys, we gonna take him, real careful like, to the next town where they have a good doctor. He'll do what he can for Reece, then we'll come back here."

"We're still gonna look for the priest?"

Toby's eyes bored into Coop. "More than ever. Reece blamed him for everything that's happened. That bastard has everything to pay for."

"Priest?" asked Arabella.

"It's a long story. I'll tell you when we get back. Now, what is this town we're headin' for?"

"It's a railroad town, or soon will be. It's called Prairie Rise."

16

The slap sounded like the crack of a whip, it was delivered with such force. Ritter's eyes watered and, staggering sideways, He gasped, "Holy shit!"

"You bastard!" she accused, her eyes blazing with anger. "You said you'd come right back."

He held up his right hand and with his left, he deftly untied his neckerchief, which he used to dab at his face. Stinging heat spread across his cheek. "Damn, you didn't have to hit me so hard."

"To hell with you, Gus Ritter. I'd beat you to death if I didn't love you so much!" She grabbed him and pressed herself into his chest. Her soft lips found his and she kissed him long and hard. When at last she pulled away, she was crying. "Don't you ever do anything like that again, you hear me?" she said, beating his chest gently with her fists.

"I do," he said and kissed her nose, "I do. And I'm sorry. But look –" he swiveled around and pointed to the young boy standing there, shivering with shock or fear, or perhaps a combination of the two – "I found this boy. Rescued him from some savages. They'd kidnapped him."

"Oh, my God," said Nati, seeing the child for the first time. As her anger subsided and the relief washed over her, she went to him. The boy recoiled, hands spread out to ward her off.

"You've frightened the hell out of him," said Ritter, wiping his nose with the neckerchief before replacing it. "His name's Jeremiah. He told me the Indians came in the night, killed his grandpa and ran off with him before his ma and some Chinaman could rescue him."

"Chinaman?" She got down on her knees, staring at the boy in his blue serge work trousers and checkered shirt. His boots were worn, his toes sticking out of the end. He looked as if he hadn't eaten or slept for at least two days. "Don't you worry none, sweetheart. I'm not really as bad as I seem."

She tried a smile but Jeremiah didn't respond. "Poor little mite, he's scared to death."

"Who wouldn't be, with a mountain lion such as yourself in front of him?"

"Shoot, Gus, I ain't no mountain lion! I ain't *that* bad."

"You're a darned sight worse, Nati." He felt his smarting cheek as if to reconfirm his words. "He'll be fine in a little while, once he realizes you're not some mad woman. How's the padre?"

"Alive." She stood up. "Just. We need to get to that town."

"It's up ahead, about half a day away. We could make it by early morning if we set off now."

"Isn't it dangerous, with them Indians everywhere?"

"From what the boy says, that Chinaman killed most of 'em. The ones who got away... Well, they won't be bothering anyone again. I reckon we're safe."

Still on her knees, Nati looked again at the boy. "A Chinaman helped you?"

At the mention of him, the boy's face brightened and he nodded enthusiastically. "He did all he could but it was my fault. I ran away. I'm sorry I did that. I am. I promise."

His eyes clouded over and his face crumpled. Clamping his hands to his face, he broke down, wailing as if pierced with pain. Nati rushed over to embrace him and this time he didn't flinch, but held onto her and poured out all his suffering and pent-up fears into her comforting arms.

Despite the early hour, the town buzzed with activity. It seemed to Ritter, as he rode beside the wagon, that the railroad never slept. Burly men moved like somnambulists, limbs heavy with fatigue, eyes red-rimmed. The garbled outpourings of a dozen different dialects and accents peppered the chilly morning air.

"I'll go ask at the sheriff's office for the address of a doctor. Will you be all right here for a moment?"

Nati nodded and patted the Winchester on her lap. "Do you really need to ask?"

"No, but there is one helluva lot of mean-looking individuals hereabouts. You keep your wits about you." He gestured towards the sheriff's office, where feeble yellow lamplight proclaimed it was occupied. "I'm right there if you need me."

She chuckled and Gus doffed his hat then eased his way across the busy street, hitched his horse to the rail and stepped up to the door. He rapped on it tentatively. There was an answering groan from within, and he pushed open the door.

The room was cramped and tiny, dominated by a desk and the uniformed man behind it. He was stretching and yawning as Gus came in. Over against the back wall, a small, iron-barred cell contained a huddled figure in dark clothes, laid out on a narrow bench.

"Sheriff ain't here," said the soldier through a second, loud, open yawn. "Holy shit, what time is it?"

"Must be around four or five, I reckon. Sun is barely up, but this place is already alive with activity."

"Yeah, well…" Standing up, the soldier moved over to the cell and peered inside. "The owners want the railroad lines down as soon as they can. I'm guarding this sonofabitch until we leave for Fort James, probably within the next hour, I shouldn't wonder." He turned his head towards Ritter and took a long time studying him. "You a lawman yourself?"

"Nope. I have a friend – a priest. He's in a real bad way and I need a doctor."

"You look like a lawman, with those guns and all."

"Well, I ain't. A doctor?"

"I wouldn't know. Like I say, my troop is leaving shortly. You'll have to ask over at the livery or one of the stores. The chandler's is more than likely open. Maybe a haberdasher's. Best try them."

Gus tipped his hat, shot one last glance into the cell and went outside again.

He stood on the boardwalk, watching disgruntled, stooped men moving with the heavy tread of the bored and weary. Not for the first time, he gave up a silent prayer of thanks that his life was not as hard as that of these men. Spotting a merchant's store directly opposite, he went across to inquire where he might find a doctor.

* * *

The man with the paunch stepped back from the bed, breathing hard. Gus and he had struggled with Father's Merry's considerable bulk, laying him out amongst clean, white sheets.

"Looks bad," said the man, leaning over to peer at the deep hatchet wounds. "They cut him up real bad. He's gonna need stitches, a lot of 'em. Before that,

I'm gonna clean his wounds and that'll put him on the ceiling with the pain." He stood up and put out his hand. "Doctor Wainright. How in hell did this happen?"

"Indians," said Ritter, shaking the small, podgy hand. "We was just setting down for supper when they came at us like devils, screaming their damned heads off."

"But you saw them off." He nodded at Ritter's guns. "You must be adept with those things."

"You could say."

"Well, you'll have to hand them in to the sheriff. There is a town ordinance. Keeps this place free from gunplay despite all the Irish, Italians and Chinese there is around here. Sooner this damned junction is fixed up, the better."

Ritter grew quiet, his attention taken up by Merry, whose breathing appeared ragged, as if he was struggling to get enough air. "Is he gonna make it?"

"Hard to say. We'll know more once I've cleaned him up and put the stitches in. I hate to mention money, but..."

Shrugging, Ritter dipped into his coat pocket. "How much are we talking, Doc?"

"Two or three hundred." He gave a lame smile. "It might increase if things don't go too well."

Sighing, Ritter peeled off the bills from his roll. "Fortunately, I have managed to acquire enough to see me through such unforeseen setbacks."

"Setbacks over what?"

Ritter smiled. "No need to trouble yourself with any of that, Doc. You just get this man straightened out – I need him alive."

He went outside and found the street considerably quieter than before. He mounted his horse and rode it back to the main street, where he found Nati perched on the buckboard of the wagon which she'd parked outside the sheriff's office. The boy sat next to her. He seemed a lot cheerier than before and grinned at Ritter's approach.

"We'll have to call back later this afternoon," said Ritter, looking down the street in the general direction of Wainright's surgery. "The doc didn't seem to offer up much hope, though."

"Oh no, Gus. This is just too awful." Biting her lip, she looked away and Ritter caught sight of Jeremiah's hand slipping inside hers. "I don't think I can take any more loss."

As he stared at her, unsure how to react, Ritter's attention was taken up by a sudden burst of activity from the opposite end of the street. A troop of United States Cavalry was approaching at a canter, a straight-backed lieutenant at the lead. At the sheriff's office, they reined in and, not more than half-a-dozen paces away, the lieutenant and his sergeant dismounted and went up to the door. The officer doffed his hat in Nati's direction and went inside.

"We should find a saloon or hotel," said Ritter, turning back to Nati. By now, she was sobbing, and Jeremiah had his arms round her shoulders. "We need to get some breakfast and rest."

"Yes," she said, sniffing loudly. She sat up and smiled at the boy. "I'm all right. Don't fret none."

"But you're not all right," said Jeremiah. "You're sad and I don't like you being sad."

"I'll be fine." She brushed away some tears with the back of her hand and went to take the reins. "Like Gus says, let's find ourselves a nice place to get us something to eat. Then we can work out how we're going to find your ma."

"I'm not sure I want to."

"Aah, don't be silly, Jeremiah, of course you do."

"No, I truly don't. I hated living in that place, with Mama drinking all the time and Grandpa beating me. Everything changed when Pa got killed." He looked around. "It was here."

"What?" said Ritter, eyes wide. "Your Pa was killed here?"

"Yessir. Right here, like I said. He was gunned down by some gunfighter."

Ritter felt himself go cold. "A gunfighter? I don't suppose you can recall his name?"

"Oh yessir, I can. It's a name I shall never forget. John Wesley Hardin."

"Oh Gus," cried Nati, "good God Almighty!"

Stunned by the news, Ritter had to hold onto the pommel of his saddle to save himself from falling. He looked into Nati's eyes, saw the alarm and concern there, and for a moment could not find the words to speak.

Behind him, raised voices accompanied the heavy stomps of booted feet as the sheriff's office door creaked open. A man boomed, "I told you two hundred, Lieutenant, but darned if I'll let this varmint go without another fifty. Your men finished off my best bourbon, damn their hides."

More scuffling.

Then Jeremiah's face grew ghastly white, the blood draining from it, his eyes almost popping.

A woman's voice sounded, harsh and bitter. "I'm coming with you. I'll see him swing, so I'll pay the damned fifty."

"Ah, ma'am, you have no need to do any such thing. It's the officer here who should—"

"Mama?"

Ritter snapped himself back into the present, caught Jeremiah's look and turned to the sheriff's office. They were all standing there. A sergeant, and the soldier he'd spoken to earlier holding the Chinaman, the Lieutenant shaking his head, the sheriff with his thumbs stuck in his belt looking stubborn and mean as hell... And a woman, the kind who made every man's head turn, with her face alive with disbelief, staring directly towards the boy.

"Jeremiah?"

They all stood stock still, as if frozen in time. Nobody moved for a few seconds. And then Jeremiah was leaping from the buckboard and the woman was running towards him. "Holy Jesus," muttered Nati.

Ritter looked and saw the woman swinging the boy around in her arms, laughing and crying. His eyes drifted beyond them to the prisoner. An Asian man. Small and wiry. It was him, the one Jeremiah had told them about. The one who had tried so hard to save the boy's life.

17

Kicking his way through the rock-strewn ground, Oscar flopped down on a large boulder and immediately regretted it. He jumped up, dusting off the seat of his pants like the proverbial scalded cat. "Holy shit, that is hot!"

The two brutish-looking soldiers accompanying the officers laughed openly. Jewson merely sighed, shook his head and led his horse across to the only piece of shade there was. The ride to this clearing had been long and laborious and all of them were tired and short-tempered.

"We need to wait a while longer," he said, pulling off his hat and wiping his soaking forehead. He stared in distaste at the sweat ring running above the brim of his Cavalry headgear. "I wish I'd told them to meet us at the fort."

"They would never have agreed to that."

Jewson gave Oscar a withering look. "I'm joking, you ass."

Not amused, Oscar tried the boulder again, this time with a good deal more care, and managed to settle himself down. "Comancheros are not known for their brevity, Captain. Neither am I."

"I don't care what they're known for. I just want the money. Higgins," he called one of the men over, "I want you to scout ahead for a mile or two and see if you can make out any sign of them."

Higgins exchanged a nervous glance with the other trooper. "Alone?"

"Yes, damn it! Leave Jones with us. Damned Comancheros should have been here well before now."

"Maybe they got into trouble?"

"*Trouble*? Men like them don't get into trouble, they *make* it. Now, move off and be quick about it."

Flicking his kepi in a poor excuse for a salute, Higgins climbed into his saddle and led his horse out of the clearing, disappearing amongst the rocky outcrops within a few paces.

Sighing, Jewson fished a cigar out of his shirt, bit off the end and studied it before sticking it into his mouth. "The shipment you managed to acquire, it was genuine?"

Oscar perked up, a deep frown creasing his face. "Genuine? What the hell do you mean by that?"

"I mean, I'm wondering why they're not here. They may be a lot of things, but they're not double-crossers. At least, not with me."

"The guns were top quality, factory-fresh Winchesters. The dynamite was crated, A-grade. I checked it all myself."

Grunting, Jewson wandered over to another rock and put one boot on it. He lit up his cigar and smoked in silence for a few moments. "Then why the hell ain't they here?"

"I don't know, but I agree with you – they wouldn't double-cross us. We're worth too much to them, supplying them with the best there is." He mopped his brow with his neckerchief. "I have to tell you, Captain, there are those back in Kansas who are growing suspicious at my repeated requisition orders. We may have to ease off for a few months."

"I told you. Two more. That's it."

"Yes, well, like I said, I feel we should—"

He got no further. Higgins came pounding into the clearing, pulling his horse up sharply in a billowing cloud of dust. Jumping down, he shot alarmed looks at each of his companions. "They're dead."

A stunned silence. A moment of disbelief. Jewson, the first to recover, went up to the soldier at a rush. "What do you mean 'dead'? Who is dead?"

"The damned Comancheros," said Higgins, wrenching his water canteen from his saddle and gulping down a huge mouthful. Gasping, he held Jewson's stare. "It's true. They were obviously ambushed or something. Wagons blown apart, bodies everywhere. I've never seen anything like it."

"Ah, Christ!" Turning away, Jewson chomped on his cigar, blowing out gouts of grey smoke. "This'll be the work of Comanches – the same damned war-party I hoped Connick would come across."

"Connick?" Oscar got up off the boulder. "What's he got to do with this?"

"Nothing, I hope."

"What the hell *is* this, Jewson?" Oscar snapped his head towards the two soldiers. "Do you two know what's going on?"

Both soldiers shook their heads. Then, without warning, Higgins drew his Colt Cavalry and aimed it directly towards his captain. "Perhaps you should explain, Cap."

"Put that damned gun away, soldier, before I—"

"Before you do what?" demanded Jones, also drawing his revolver.

"Explain to us what the hell is going on," said Oscar, stepping between the two soldiers.

Jewson's eyes flipped from one pointed gun to the next and swallowed hard. "There's nothing to tell."

"Well, it doesn't seem like nothing to me," said Oscar. "We had a deal, Captain. An agreement. I'd supply the weapons from U.S. Army stores, and you'd supply the contacts. You said you knew these men… that you had dealt with them before."

"I do – I mean, I *did*. Sending Connick out to track down those Comanches was a simple insurance policy, nothing more. He's bright, eager and ambitious. He's only been at the fort for a month and already he's asking questions. I hoped he'd run into trouble, get himself killed. Looks like it might have been him doing the killing."

"Who were the guns for?" asked Higgins.

"Comanches, I guess. Why?"

"Because most of them were lying around on the ground useless, destroyed in the explosion. There's no dynamite, either."

Oscar gasped and passed a trembling hand over his face. "Jeez, if those Comanch believe they've been double-crossed… Boys, this is not the place to be right now. Captain," he pointed at Jewson, "if you're lying to us, then so help me—"

"I'm not lying, you puffed-up shopkeeper. And don't threaten me. If Connick attacked that Comanchero payload, he's more than likely done for the Comanches, too. Which doesn't give us much time."

"Much time for what?"

"To get back to the fort. If he links any of us to this deal, he'll put us under arrest. He'll have the proof to do so if he finds me absent from my post. Boys, put your goddamned guns away and let's get the hell out of here."

Without a word of protest, the two soldiers did so and walked off towards their waiting horses.

Oscar saw it first, a soundless cry coming from his open mouth.

Grinning, Jewson shot the two soldiers in the back with his own Colt Cavalry, four bullets, sent across the space of a few feet, smashing into their spinal columns, flinging them face-first to the ground.

"You slimy bastard," said the Captain, turning the gun on Oscar, who stood whimpering, jowls wobbling. "Nobody talks to me the way you did."

Oscar's hands moved slowly skywards. "Captain, just hold on. We was all confused, is all. I never doubted you, not once, but something happened to those Comancheros."

"It was Connick, for sure. No one else could have done it, and he'll be heading back to Fort James even now. But you've given me an idea, Oscar. A great idea."

"I – I don't understand."

"You and those two," he nodded towards the dead soldiers, "you set the whole thing up. I followed you, found out about your dealings with the Comancheros, and when I tried to arrest you, you made a run for it." He smiled. "I was forced to shoot you dead, along with your fellow-conspirators."

"Don't be such a fool. No one will believe you, Jewson. We had a good deal going here. We can still make a lot of money from this!"

"No. Connick has rumbled the whole thing. I'm cutting loose, with the money we already have. I'll take your cut, you flathead."

"You can't! Damn it all, Jewson, we can make ourselves a small fortune from this, you said so yourself."

"With your cut, I already have a tidy sum." His smile grew broader. "This has actually all turned out for the best."

"No. No, it hasn't. We can—"

The single gunshot rang out as loud as a cannon blast and Oscar crumpled to the ground lifeless, to join the others.

Jewson holstered his gun. Shaking his head, he crossed to the horses and calmed them with tender words and gentle strokes of their necks. He gathered them close, tying their reins together in preparation to ride out.

Taking one last glance around the small clearing where the three dead bodies lay sprawled, he hauled himself into the saddle and went to turn his horse around.

Only then did he catch sight of the mounted figures standing in a line across the highest hilltop, watching him in silence.

There were at least a dozen of them.

Comanches.

Cursing, Jewson spurred his horse, making to charge out of the clearing and beat his hasty retreat to Fort James.

But four remaining warriors from the war-party blocked his path. They sat astride their mounts, just as their companions on the ridge did, silent, their eyes full of hatred. Jewson screamed, "I didn't do it! It wasn't me!"

No one answered.

In continuing silence, three of the warriors nocked arrows. They took their time. The outcome was without question.

18

Han stood staring, a self-conscious smile playing at the corners of his mouth.

Pressed against her bosom, Jeremiah turned his head and gazed at the Okinawan. "What are you doing here?"

"Never mind about that, son," said the tall, kind-looking Cavalry officer, patting him on the shoulder. "I'm taking this is your boy, ma'am, the one you told me the Comanches had kidnapped?"

Smiling, Susannah kissed the top of Jeremiah's head, the relief gushing out of her. "Yes. My dear, sweet boy. Come back to me."

In that moment, it seemed as if reality had brought everything back into sharp focus and Jeremiah, sniffing loudly, pushed himself away. The joy he'd felt at seeing his mother alive and well subsided, as the memories of that awful night returned. "Ma, why didn't you try and rescue me?"

She gaped at him and looked across his shoulder to the stranger standing next to a wagon.

"His name's Gus," said Jeremiah. "*He* saved me."

"Well then," spoke up the sheriff, who'd watched the whole exchange with seeming interest, "it seems this fine lady owes you a great deal. What's your name, fella?"

"Ritter."

The lawman seemed to chew over the name for a moment or two, flicking through his vast mental records of the wanted. Finding nothing which registered, he nodded his head, pointing towards Ritter's guns. "I'll be asking you to hand those in, son."

"We'll be leaving directly."

"Even so."

Ritter nodded and the slim, smoky-eyed woman, sitting on the wagon buck-board, handed him her Winchester. Unbuckling his gun belt, Ritter stepped up close to the gaggle of people and handed the weapons over. Arms fully laden, the sheriff dipped back into his office, returning a moment later to see Ritter's eyes resting on the Asian. "Sheriff, I reckon this here lady owes this fella a helluva lot of thanks, too."

"What's that you say?" snapped the young officer.

The woman blanched.

"The boy told it, every word of it," continued Ritter, studying the handcuffs snapped tightly shut around the slight Asian's wrists. "This here gentleman did all that he could to save them from the attack. Lost his friend in the process."

"That can't be," said the officer. He turned and looked at Susannah, then the boy. "Can it?"

"I watched him from my room," said Jeremiah. He smiled towards the Asian, who remained impassive, almost resigned to his fate. "I saw him fight those varmints, but there were too many and when the big old fella got shot with arrows, I made a run for it out of my bedroom window. Stupid, I know, but I wanted to try and get a horse and ride away." He looked at his mother. "I wasn't being a coward or nothing, Ma, but I was sorely afraid. There were so many of 'em. I'm sorry."

"Is what the boy says the truth, ma'am?"

Susannah, her face a ghostly white, managed to shake her head. Just once. She stood silent for a long time, gathering herself until, with the colour return-ing to her cheeks, she pulled herself up straight and glared at her son with brew-ing anger. "No. No, it wasn't like that. The Chinaman brought them, brought all them red-devils just like I said. He led those savages to my home."

"No he didn't, Ma. You wanted to shoot him, shoot him dead as soon as he arrived. You were calling him names and all sorts of things."

"No, I... Jeremiah, you stop with your tittle-tattle now. This man, he's re-sponsible for Grandpappy's killing, and your pa's, too. That's right," she turned her wide eyes towards the officer, "it was him that lured my husband here, to this town, to meet up with his partner in crime. They tricked him, you see. They contrived to murder him. Both of 'em. That Hardin and him."

"Hardin?"

They all looked at Ritter, noting the urgency in his voice.

Clearing his throat, the sheriff leaned across and took the handcuff key from the sergeant's fist. Inserting it into the lock, he released the Asian from his manacles. "If what I'm hearing is correct, there was a killing out here a few months back. Some say it was Hardin, the gunfighter, who did it, but witnesses were mighty scant in coming forward. There was certainly no mention of no Chinaman involved."

"I am Okinawan, and my name is—"

"Han," said Jeremiah and he pushed his way through the men to stand in front of the small Okinawan. He held out his hand. "I never did get to thank you for what you tried to do. If I'd have stayed in my room, I reckon them varmints never would have taken me."

Taking the boy's hand, Han smiled at him with real affection.

"I think we need to reconsider this entire situation, Lieutenant," said the sheriff. "We can talk about it in my office, make it all official, like."

"I'm due back at Fort James. I need to make my report." He looked at Ritter. "You saved the lad?"

Ritter nodded, his thoughts elsewhere.

"He killed 'em all," said Jeremiah. "I ain't ever seen gunplay like it. He shot 'em all dead, quick as a blink in the sunlight."

"Is that so?" asked the officer, staring hard at the boy.

"Yes it is, Mr Lieutenant, sir. Every one of 'em."

Reaching what appeared some form of internal decision, the officer turned to Ritter. "Then you've saved me a job, sir. I'm grateful to you – my men, too. There's nothing we hate more than coming up against Comanch."

"A-men to that," said the sergeant.

"Let the prisoner go, sheriff. I'll tie up any paperwork back at the Fort then let you have a copy. After that, we can—"

"*Are you mad?*" screeched Susannah, utterly out of control now, gripping the front of the officer's shirt and tugging at him. "You can't let him go, Lieutenant Connick, *you can't!*" She was shouting, her voice raw with panic. Passers-by stopped and stared, many of them looking startled, some afraid of the woman's frenzy. She was shaking Connick hard. "You can't! For the love of God, you have to take him to the fort, you have to—"

"Ma'am, *please.* There is no call for any of this. After your son's and this good man's testimonies, I can't keep this gentleman detained. You have done him a grave disservice, for reasons I do not understand. Now please, let me go!"

She did. But not in the way anyone expected. In a blur, she made a grab for Connick's service revolver and jerked it from the holster. She stepped away, holding the gun in both hands, easing back the hammer. Everyone nearby gave an audible gasp, arms reaching up, faces agog.

"Now ma'am, you take it easy," said the sheriff in a strained voice, his arms outstretched.

Everyone could see the fury in the woman's eyes. She took another step back. "That bastard Chinaman, he's the Devil, you hear me! He tried to rape me, did I tell you that? Can't you see it, see it in his eyes? Eh? Tell me you can see it. I can see it. You all can see it, can't you!"

"Ma," said Jeremiah, taking a step forward. Tears tumbled down his cheeks as his little voice wailed, "Ma, don't do this."

"You keep that shut, Jeremiah! I've told you, told you more than once. You don't keep it shut, I'll get Grandpa to take his belt to you, you see if I don't."

"Ma," he said, pressing his fingers into his eyes, "Ma, don't. Grandpa's dead. Can't you remember, Ma?"

She shook her head, eyes fixed on the Okinawan. "It's all your fault! Ever since you came into my life, everything has gone wrong. You heathen, bringing your Hindu rantings with you. I'm going to kill you, you bastard!"

As she took another step back, her heel slipped off the edge of the board-walk and she toppled backwards, the gun going off with a huge boom. Arms flapping in a wild, desperate parody of someone attempting to fly, she hit the ground with a dull thud. Soldiers rushed to her, wrestled her into submission and retrieved the revolver. Connick, for one, looked very relieved.

"She's completely mad," said the young lieutenant. He turned to the sheriff for confirmation. "Mad."

"It happens." The sheriff ruffled Jeremiah's hair as the boy stood there, hands clamped to his face, sobbing uncontrollably. "I think this young fella needs some looking after."

"We'll do it," said Ritter's female companion.

"That's kind of you, ma'am. Thank you."

Saluting him smartly, a trooper handed Connick his revolver. He checked it and slipped it back into the holster, this time making doubly-sure the flap was closed. "She needs a doctor." Two troopers held Susannah, who sagged heavy and defeated in their arms. "With extended rest and medication, she might get better."

"Who knows?" The sheriff ran his tongue around his mouth. "I could let our doc take a look. Of course, it'll cost you."

"*Me?*" Connick looked around him in desperation. "What the hell has any of this got to do with me?"

Pointing to the young officer's holster, the sheriff looked grave. "The fact that she could so easily take your gun shows a grave contempt for your responsibilities as an officer of the United States Government, Lieutenant. It really is my duty to make a full report of what happened here..." He let his words hang in the air for a moment, before adding, "But, of course, one or two details might be omitted... for the right price."

"Damn your hide," said Connick, reaching inside his shirt.

"Yes. And the rest of me, no doubt." He winked. "Let's say a round three hundred."

19

Francis wandered into town mid-morning, his backside raw from the long ride. Reining in outside the sheriff's office, he eased himself out of the saddle, groaning as he stretched out his back. Around him, townsfolk idled by. Within their number wandered a great many worn-out-looking workers, hands black with toil, faces ingrained with fatigue. He wished he was back in Archangel, sitting in his easy chair, supper on the boil, his wife easing away his pains. For too long he had ridden across endless plains, tracking the wanted, the escaped, the desperate. What he yearned for now, more than anything, was peace. He hoped that what he was about to do would bring him some semblance of that. He rapped on the door and went inside.

The sheriff was talking to another man, their heads down, poring over various pieces of paper. He looked up as Francis stepped closer. The old tracker gave a smile and pulled off his hat. "'Morning, sheriff."

"Howdy. What can I do for you?"

"I have some information which I need you to wire across to Huntsville, Texas. It concerns someone who is of interest to the authorities of several states."

"Oh?" The sheriff shot a glance to the man beside him, who shrugged and considered Francis with his piercing blue eyes. "This here is an associate of mine, all the way from El Paso. Might be the person who you speak of would be of interest to him, also."

"Could be."

"I'm a constable out of El Paso, here to serve papers on certain desperadoes. My name is John Selman," said the big man, pushing the pile of papers aside. "Who is this person of interest, friend, and how would you be knowing of someone who is so well known to state authorities?"

"I met him by sheer fate in the town of Saint Angelo, a fearful place full of dead people." He shuddered as he recalled what had befallen him there. "We were on the trail of a killer. Marshal Climes formed a posse out of Archangel and headed south, and I aided him, me being a tracker and all."

"A tracker? Of men?"

"I tracked for the Army during the Indian Wars."

The two lawmen exchanged a glance. "Seems like we're forever having those," said the sheriff.

"So, who is this person, friend?"

"His name is John Wesley Hardin."

Selman's expression changed from polite indifference to intense interest. "Hardin? Weasel of a guy, drooping moustache, totes a brace of revolvers?"

"That just about fits him to a tee, constable. He did not shy away from telling me of his past indiscretions, in particular the shooting of a deputy, for which crime he wishes to throw himself upon the mercy of the court. It is his contention that he has been wrongly accused."

"That comes as no surprise to me," said Selman, giving a wry smile. "Nothing John Wesley does is ever his fault. So he has made his way across to Huntsville?"

"That is what I wish you to convey to the authorities there. I am afeared he may be gunned down before he ever gets to court."

"More than likely. The bastard has a queue of people more than a mile long, all out for retribution. He is a murdering sonofabitch and there are a good many folk who would dearly like to put him in the ground."

"We have one such here," said the sheriff. "Goes by the name of Ritter. Not sure if that's his name for real, but he certainly did not take kindly to the mention of Hardin's name when he heard it. He handed in his guns without a word, but he strikes me as a man well capable of using them if the cause arose."

"Your instigation of local by-laws which restrict the use of firearms has proved mighty successful," said Selman, "and it could be something I may try to introduce into El Paso, now that I have my own deputy. He, too, is a man who has been wronged by Hardin."

"Well, I have not been so wronged," said Francis. He spoke calmly, but inwardly, he was wondering what further horrors he might hear about the gunfighter if he stayed in the sheriff's office any longer. "I need to find a place to put down my head. I may well seek out this man called Ritter. Perhaps my words will bring him some comfort, knowing that Hardin will undoubtedly be brought to justice."

"It may be your news will set him on a new course to Huntsville, to confront the bastard himself. You'll find him at the Longhorn Hotel, end of Mainstreet. He's staying there for a night or two with his woman, some kid they have adopted, and a Chinaman by the name of Han."

"Sounds more of a family man than someone who wants to go up against Hardin."

"Oh, he'll go up against him all right. May well come out on top, too, if I'm any judge of character."

Francis repositioned his hat and turned to go.

"Oh," put in the sheriff quickly, "I'll be taking your guns, if you're planning on staying for more than five minutes."

Francis stopped, turned and unbuckled his belt.

20

"I wish I had my gun."

Unperturbed, Han gave a small shrug. "It does not matter."

"It might if there's trouble," said Ritter. He rolled himself a cigarette and turned his attention to the twin-story whorehouse across the street. It was late afternoon and it was the third such establishment they had visited. There remained just one more after this. Options were running thin and Han, growing more agitated with each failed discovery, had taken on a haunted look, forever fidgeting, wringing his hands, sucking in his bottom lip.

"Listen, if we don't find her, there are other towns," he said, hoping to lift the Okinawan's spirits.

"Railroad towns? How many more, do you think?"

"Lots."

"Yes. But we know that in this one, somewhere, there are Asian girls."

"Asian girls are everywhere else, too. No offence, but they are the current chosen flavour. We could be making tracks all the way back to Kansas, perhaps even beyond. The railroads are cutting their way right across the plains. Even the Indians can't stop 'em."

"But this is what they call a junction." Han allowed his breath to trickle out in a long sigh. "She has to be here."

"Let's hope so." Ritter blew out a long stream of smoke. "We'll have to move fast. Once night falls, this town will be alive with drunken rail workers looking for a fight, as well as a piece of ass." He caught Han's vicious glare. "No offence."

"We follow the same routine as before."

"Guess so, although I'm just about up to my limit in whisky. I'll try beer this time."

With that, they crossed the road, dodging the covered wagons, buggies and horses which trailed backwards and forwards. Keeping their eyes fixed on the swing doors, they went inside.

Late afternoon or not, the place appeared busy, a low hum of conversation filling the wide room. In the far corner, a man was lifting the lid of the piano. Next to him lounged a pale-skinned woman, her waist squeezed impossibly tight in a scarlet bodice with purple frills around the shoulders and neck. Black hair fell in ringlets to her narrow shoulders, their alabaster skin shimmering in the thick fug of stale cigar smoke and unwashed bodies. She turned around, smiling, and her eyes locked onto Ritter, causing his stomach to somersault, his loins to stir. "My God…"

Unable to avert his eyes, he watched her, mesmerized, as she advanced towards him, swerving around the tables, giving the occasional grin, wink or flick of hair to the customers. One made a grab for her shapely behind and received a slap for his efforts. Everyone laughed.

"Howdy, stranger," she said, breathing over him, the smell of expensive French perfume floating into his nostrils. Closing his eyes, Ritter luxuriated in the aroma, wanting it to remain with him forever. Opening his eyes again, he found her still there, this vision of exquisite loveliness, the promise of sexual satisfaction so real, so urgent. "Can I get you anything?"

As if on cue, the piano started up. Several men cheered and one of them attempted to sing, his toneless efforts soon quashed by angry rebukes. More laughter. She tossed back her hair and Ritter gulped. "I reckon."

Her smile widened. She took his hand and studied his fingers. "I'll help you unwind, but we will take a bath first. You've been on the range for a long while. You a cowboy?"

Somewhere beyond this aura of wild, illicit sex, a figure flittered on the periphery of his vision. He blinked, pulling himself clear of the woman's seductive power, and saw Han glowering at him.

"No, I… Hey," he laughed, gently drawing back his hand. "I, er, don't wish to sound ungrateful or nothing, ma'am, but… well, my tastes tend to be for the more Asian kind of girl."

If she were offended, she didn't show it. She tilted her head, her eyes smouldering with a tinge of excitement. "Mmm. Mine, too. She's a sweet young thing. You've heard of her, from your friends?"

He stood and stared, barely able to breathe. Han, behind her, took a step closer, his open mouth trembling. "Yes, yes I have. Sweet."

"Very sweet. For a just a little more, we could both entertain you. I like the look of you, stranger. There's something… Who, or what are you?"

"A pilgrim, just passing through." He saw the twinkle of amusement in her eyes and tapped the shirt pocket beneath his vest. "I'm here to spend time and money before I move on."

"Really?" Her fingers crept like a spider across his chest. She felt the bulge of banknotes and smiled again. "Well, like I say, we can all have fun together. The three of us."

"Four."

"Eh?"

"There's my friend." He nodded to Han and she turned, giggling. "You did say you like Asians!"

"I sure did. My, he looks nothing like any Asian man I've ever seen."

"That's because he's not. He's special."

"Well… Mr Whatever-your-name-is."

"Bisby. This is my friend, Chan."

"Well, Mr Bisby, my name is Lucille. I'll get Millie, our lovely little Chinese girl, to run us an extra big bath."

Some while later, Ritter and Han stood in a spacious bedroom. A set of tables with wash basins ran under the window and two unlit oil lamps flanked the impressively sized bed with its turned-back satin sheets. Apart from the main door, there was another, which led into an adjoining room into which the lovely Lucille had disappeared.

"This cannot be the place where my sister Miyoko was taken. She is not Chinese. Let's go."

He went to move and Ritter caught him by the arm. "All Asians are called Chinese, friend. Let's just wait and see."

"I don't like this. Why is this woman so desperate to get us up here?"

"Maybe she likes us."

"She's a whore. 'Like' has nothing to do with it."

"Well, maybe it's my particular charms." He chuckled and patted his pocket. "Got the bulk of this from taking down a pair of individuals called Burbank. Two brothers, wanted for robbing banks and a railroad or two. Best day's work I ever did."

"You took them in?"

"I shot 'em both dead in a saloon back in Denver. They had a price on their fat heads as big as one of them steam locomotives they held up. Fifteen thousand dollars."

Han whistled. "Enough money to retire on, maybe."

"Maybe. But I'm not about to retire yet. Not until I'm done with John Wesley. After Merry's fixed up, I'm making my way to a little place east of here. The good padre seems to think that's where he'll be. He has a girl there."

"Your friend the priest. He's in a bad way."

"My only hope is that he'll live long enough to show me where that town is. Then I'll do what I need to do. My bankroll is dwindling fast. One or two jobs after I've put Hardin away, and *then* I'll retire."

The door opened and Lucille came in, that perfect smile fixed permanently on her perfect face.

Neither Ritter nor Han joined her.

Stepping out from behind her came two men. She did not flinch as they filled the room. They were big men, sporting big guns. The man on the right side held a sawn-off shotgun, levelled at Ritter, whilst his companion, older and fuller around the waist, pointed a black revolver at the Okinawan. "My good companions here will cover you whilst I relieve you of that money," Lucille said. "One move and they'll blow you to kingdom come."

And then, for the first time, her smile faded, replaced by a cruel sneer and a small pocket Navy Colt in her fist. She moved closer.

Han gave a tiny yelp.

They all stopped, surprised at Han's reaction. Ritter, shooting him a glance, followed the Okinawan's gaze into the adjoining room and the young Asian girl standing there next to a large tin bath.

It all happened so quickly then, too quickly for Ritter to fully register what was happening. Han moved, his right arm streaking through the air. His elbow cracked into Lucille's jaw and he turned her in his arms, rolling with her to the right. Locked together, her wrist snapped. She screamed, the gun dropped from her fingers and went clattering to the floor.

One of the men squealed. The one with the revolver. Confused, as everything was happening so fast, he hesitated and Han was on him, sweeping the man's leg from under him, spilling him downwards.

The one with the shotgun turned, easing back the hammers. But who to shoot? They were all too close. The spread from the blast would be indiscriminate, possibly even killing Lucille.

Ritter rolled also. No time to think now… No time to consider the error of firing a gun in this town, a town in which guns were outlawed. He swept up Lucille's little cut-down Colt Navy and aimed it at the shotgun-bearer's head. "Drop it!"

Lucille was screaming, writhing on the ground, left hand clamped over her broken, flapping wrist, the skin already swollen, the bone protruding against the flesh but not piercing it. The other gunman was in some sort of headlock and Han had the man's revolver pointing towards the man with the shotgun. "Do it!" he said.

Fortunately for them all, the man did so, bending at his knees to place the sawn-off with almost reverential slowness on the floor. Ritter, the Colt Navy still aimed unerringly towards the man's head, slunk forwards and picked up the sawn-off shotgun. He disengaged the hammers and stood to his full height. Stuffing the Colt into his waistband, he deftly reversed the shotgun and rammed the stock hard into the man's jaw, knocking him backwards against the far wall in a mess of broken teeth, cheekbone and blood. In silence, he slid to the floor in a heap and remained still.

The other man bleated something incoherent. Han released him and then snap-kicked the man in the head. He flopped sideways, eyes rolling. He might have been dead. From Ritter's perspective, the man wouldn't be getting up anytime soon.

Han, for his part, had other things on his mind – his sister Miyoko, standing with a look of total disbelief on her beautiful face.

She was crying as she fell into her brother's arms.

21

Nati was sitting at a table finishing an afternoon meal when Ritter came through the door, pausing only to acknowledge the barkeeper's wave of welcome before he sat down, breathing hard.

"What's happened?"

She knew him well enough to read the signs. Indeed, from his agitated state, anyone with fairly good eyesight could have seen it. The sweat glistened across his forehead, his eyes darted, his mouth chewed at his own cheeks.

"We have to leave. And we have to leave now."

She considered her half-eaten meal and sat back. Next to her, Jeremiah paused in the action of putting spoon into mouth.

The other man who sat at the table, mopping his bowl with a hunk of bread, stopped in mid-action.

And that's when Ritter noticed Nati was not alone, and he stared at her with the unspoken question.

"This gentleman is out of Archangel. You remember Archangel, don't you, Gus? What happened there?"

Shaking his head, Ritter turned from her gaze. The man appeared old, tuckered-out. He also bore scars. Fresh. As if he'd taken a beating.

"I understand your good wife had some trouble there."

Blinking, Ritter shook his head again, the fog in his brain refusing to lift. "Eh? What?"

"Florence!" snapped Nati, throwing down her spoon. "You remember her, don't you, Gus?"

"Of course I do. What are you—?"

"Where the hell have you been all day? I woke up to find you gone and now here you are, out of breath, like you been in a fight. You been in a fight, Gus?"

"No, I..." He looked again at the old man. "You've brought news from Archangel?"

"Lots," he said, picking up a napkin to dab at his mouth, his meal now forgotten. The air around the table was tense. "I can tell you later, as I'm thinking you two are in need of some private conversation."

"No," said Nati, "you tell him, like you told me. Then me and him will talk."

Ritter blew out a breath. "There ain't no mystery, Nat, just—"

"Jeremiah went looking for you on his way to see his ma over at the doctor's. He came back all upset. Said he'd seen you and Han going into a whorehouse. You want to explain that to me, Gus?"

"Nati, it's not what you—"

"Like I say," put in the old man, "I'll come back. Son, you and me should go for a walk someplace." He winked towards Jeremiah.

"*Hell's bells*!" shouted Ritter, his fist coming down hard on the table, sending cutlery and crockery jumping into the air to return with a crash. "We went looking for Han's sister, goddamn it! We been looking all day. We found her in some sleazy place where the Madame made a play for my money. Tried to rob us with two fat guys packing guns. Han put them down like nothing I've never seen, and we left 'em tied up and broken in the room. Han is fetching our wagon to get us out of this place before they come looking for us. Only good thing is, he found his sister."

Breathing hard, he glared at each of them in turn, finally settling on Nati who, shocked and speechless, brought her hands up in surrender. "There. You satisfied? Goddamn it, can we *please* just hear what this old-timer has to say before we leave?"

The old-timer blew out his cheeks. "I'll be quick, if that's all right with you."

"Just get on with it," said Ritter, reaching over to help himself to the man's forgotten bread.

"Archangel has changed some since you and this good lady were last there. The Scrimshaws have all gone. Last I heard, Reece was the only one left alive. He's down here, looking to go to Mexico. We found out he's looking for the same man we are – by *we*, I mean a small posse led by Marshal Climes out of Cheyenne. We were looking for the killer of Doc Monroe. Doc Monroe had been tending Toby Scrimshaw and we believed the man who beat him may well have shot him dead. A priest, so we understand. Well, Climes and the others are all dead now. The Scrimshaws did it, I reckon, before they set off on the trail again. God knows where they are now. On my way here, I met up with a gunfighter. John Wesley Hardin."

A piece of uneaten bread, in the act of being popped into Ritter's mouth, dropped from the bounty-hunter's fingers. "Hardin, you say?"

"Sheriff here tells me you is looking for him. Well, I have to tell you, he is going back to Texas to give himself in to the law. Seems he has a desire to end his old ways and wishes to repent."

"*Repent*? A rabid killer like him don't repent, old-timer."

"That's as maybe, but he is set to do it. Huntsville. That's where you'll find him."

"Then that's where I'll head for."

"He told me something else, too… something which I've figured out, despite not understanding it fully when he told me the story."

Ritter stared, urging him to continue.

"He told me the story of a young man he'd tried to save. A young man set upon by a band of scurrilous troublemakers. A young man out escorting his bride-to-be. Seems they took exception to the way this young man tried to protect his fiancée. Trouble started, and it was Hardin who stepped in and settled it, putting the leader of those braggarts into the ground. But before he died, this piece of work put a bullet through the young man's heart – the young man who Hardin had wanted to help."

"Gus?"

Nati's voice seemed to come from far away.

Not hearing, not wishing to, Ritter pushed back his chair and wandered outside as if in a daze.

The world went on all around him but, for Gus Ritter, his mind turned on one single thought.

He'd got it wrong. All these months. Years. His purpose, his reason. His desire to kill one man, John Wesley Hardin. It was all based on nothing but a lie.

In the slow, dwindling end of that long day, he held onto the door of the hotel and wept.

22

Easing the wagon to the side of the street, Toby jumped down and checked Reece before calling on the doctor. The first passer-by he'd asked knew Dr Wainright's address, which was a godsend. The journey had taken nearly two days, far longer than Arabella had said it would. With the going so painstakingly slow, Toby, his concentration locked on the trail as he avoided every deep rut and large stone, felt physically and mentally drained. But here they were at last. The day was slipping into evening but the streets were still busy. A railroad town, Arabella had told him. Not the kind of place to linger in for too long.

Rapping on the surgery door, Toby beckoned his companions to form a ring around the open wagon, depriving the curious of a close look at the grotesque thing lying there. Reece had barely moved throughout the journey, just emitting the occasional groan through his lipless mouth, those white eyes staring, wet and unblinking.

The door wrenched open and a man in a stained white shirt and braces peered out. "I've closed for the day," he began, but Toby was not listening. Without a word, he took the good doctor by the arm and pulled him out into the street. Before he could utter any kind of objection, Toby swung him towards the vision lying prone on his back, burned to a crisp. "Oh, my sweet Jesus."

"Tend to him," said Toby in a shaking voice, surprising himself with the depth of his grief. If he lost his brother, what was the point? How could he go on living?

Turning his horrified face away, the doctor shook his head, mumbling, "He's beyond any help I can give him. Dear God, man, what happened to him?"

"You don't need to bother yourself with the details," said Toby, drawing his gun and pressing the muzzle against the doctor's temple. "Fix him, or I'll fix you." To give greater credence to his words, he snapped back the hammer.

Quaking, the doctor's hands came up. "I... I'm not sure I can."

Toby nodded. Once. "You can."

Slowly recovering some degree of self-control, Wainright gestured to the men. "Bring him in as carefully as you can. Take him straight through to the back. I have another patient, but there are two beds."

"We'll make room," said Toby, uncocking the revolver and returning it to the holster. He waved to the others. They took up their original stations, one at each corner of the tarpaulin, and they carefully lifted Reece from the flat-bed wagon. Toby watched them, gritting his teeth. Then he reached into the wagon and pulled out a Winchester.

If he'd have paused and glanced towards the end of the street, he would have noticed a slightly built man of indeterminate age staring with open interest at what was happening. But Toby saw nothing, all his concentration fixed on the men struggling with Reece's charred body as they took him into the doctor's surgery.

"There were five of them," said Francis, standing in the doorway of Ritter's room.

Busying herself with what few possessions they had, Nati looked up. "We have no time for this."

Ritter nodded in agreement. "She's right. I'll go across to the doc's and pay him enough to make sure the padre gets better, but we can't take him with us."

"I have a bad feeling about this, especially after what happened to your sister, Miss Natalie."

She paused in the act of rolling up a bed blanket and stared. Next to her, Jeremiah sat swinging his legs, seeming unconcerned. Nati mussed his hair and said to Francis, "What are you talking about?"

Francis drew a deep breath. "I thought you should know, that is all. When I saw the big one pulling his gun, I knew they were not ordinary men."

"They could be anyone," said Ritter, "but I'll go and check all the same."

"You're not understanding my meaning," said Francis. "I recognized the big one. Hell, anyone out of Archangel would know him."

Nati's voice, like ice, seemed to chill the very air. "Who was it?"

"It was Toby Scrimshaw."

* * *

"Put him down as gently as you can," instructed the doctor, indicating the vacant bed with a trembling hand. As the men squeezed through the room, one of them inadvertently kicked the next bed and the man lying there moaned. Toby shot him a glance and noticed the bandages that were swathed like an Ancient Egyptian mummy around his head. "He got burnt too?"

"No, Indians. Hacked through his cheek and jawbone."

Wincing, Toby nodded to the others. "Wait outside, boys. We'll wander over to the saloon in a short while, get ourselves some refreshment." They shuffled out, happy to be away from that place, their spirits rising at the prospect of long-hoped-for drinks.

"Seems like you specialize in no-hopers, Doc," Toby said.

"Hardly." He looked again at Reece. "I'm going to have to get someone to help."

"No. No one else."

He turned, meeting Toby's hard look. "I must. I have an assistant, a nurse who occasionally drops in to help. I'll need her. Otherwise," he shot another look at Toby's stricken brother, "he won't make it. Even if he does…" a heavy, defeated look spread over the doctor's face, "he'll never be the same again. He'll need constant, twenty-four-hour care. I've seen burns before, but never anything like this. It's a miracle he's still alive."

"He has my father's woman, back at the ranch. Manuela. She'll tend to him, don't worry about that."

"He can't be moved, not for weeks. Maybe months."

"I'll pay you, if that's what's worrying you. Just you make sure you fix him."

"I shall do my best."

Nodding, Toby turned away and caught sight of a brown, blood-soaked garment hanging from a peg behind the door. A frown creased his face and he went up to it, feeling the coarse cloth between finger and thumb. "What's this?"

"Eh?"

Snapping his head round, Toby pointed the Winchester directly towards Wainright. "I asked you what this is."

The doctor blanched and raised his hands in sudden fear. "It's his." He nodded towards the other patient. "I told you, he was cut up real bad and I—"

"I couldn't give a good goddamn about what's wrong with him. Just tell me who he is!"

"A priest," blurted the doctor, "he's a priest, that's all."

"Take off his bandages."

"What? I can't, he's recovering from—"

The lever engaged the first round, Toby's grip on the gun solid and unwavering. Narrowing his eyes, Toby hissed, "Take off his bandages and take them off *now* – I want to get a good look at his face."

On his way down the main street, Ritter spotted Han, sitting on the wagon buckboard. As he approached, he saw his sister hiding behind him, her frightened eyes peering out through the canvas opening.

"We've got trouble."

"What sort? The sheriff?"

"A lot worse. I need your help, Han."

"You do not need to ask, my friend."

Ritter nodded, patting the Pocket Navy concealed under his shirt. "I have five shots. It's not going to be enough."

"Then let us get to it." Han swiveled around and smiled at his sister. "I will not be long, Miyoko."

Francis had positioned himself opposite the doctor's office. He gave a long sigh as the other walked up to him. "Jesus, I thought you'd never get here. They're inside. Toby and four others."

"Merry's in there," said Ritter. "If Toby sees him… Han, you stand beside the door. There's gonna be shooting, but any you can drop is gonna make the whole situation a damn sight easier."

"Who is Merry?" asked Francis, as the others strode across the street.

"A friend," called back Ritter, tugging the Pocket Navy from his waistband.

The men who emerged from within the doctor's surgery were armed, but they were not expecting to see another man standing before them, gun in hand.

No words were needed and they spread out, wary, ready.

There were four of them, all well schooled in the art of gunplay. Already, they were positioning themselves, recognizing something in Ritter – the way he stood, the glint in his eye, they way his body was coiled, ready to spring into action.

But, before any of them could react and draw their guns from their holsters, the first cowhand received a bullet through the head. Somebody shouted out something. They tried to bring their weapons to bear. The one holding the scatter gun took two in the chest, flipping him over. A mistake. A costly one,

Ritter realized, but he had no choice now. He shot the third cowhand as he attempted to roll out of range. The bullet went through the man's temple, the ghastly consequence being a right eye blown out of its socket, to hang like a trail of egg white dangling from the broken shell.

Ritter had no more bullets. And the remaining man, flattened against the wall, comatose with fear, recovered, scarcely able to believe his luck, and pulled his gun from its holster.

Han hit him hard, putting the man's body into shock, turning legs to rubber. The second blow crushed his larynx, killing him before he hit the ground.

A shape emerged from the shadow of the doorway – a huge, lumbering man who moved with surprising speed.

"Sonofabitch!" said Toby. He smashed the stock of his Winchester into Han's head, dropping the Okinawan like a stone.

The big man stood in the doorway, breathing hard, shaking his head in disbelief at what he saw. All of his men. All dead.

He turned his face to Ritter, standing in a half-crouch, a resigned look on his face.

"Who the fuck are you?"

"Did you kill him?"

Toby blinked, not fully understanding the question. He worked the lever and brought it to eye-level. "I knocked him down, but I'll kill him and you, you bastard, in a second or two."

"I meant the priest."

A flicker of understanding played around Toby's eyes. "You his friend?"

"I asked, did you kill him?"

"Not yet, you bastard. You interrupted me. But I will, after I've finished you."

Ritter never did fully understand where she got the gun from. It may have been from one of the dead bodies, or it may have been that she had kept it concealed from John Selman when they first arrived. Such thoughts didn't concern him very much when Nati put her first bullet into the back of Toby's calf.

Screaming, the big man hit the boardwalk with a terrible crash, the weight of him almost breaking the wooden slats. He writhed, blood spewing between the fingers clutching at his destroyed leg muscle.

Ritter ran forward, sweeping up Toby's rifle.

"No!"

He stopped dead at the sound of Nati's voice and snapped his head round to see her walking towards him, with all the nonchalance of someone out for a Sunday stroll. She handed him her revolver and took the Winchester. She engaged another cartridge into the chamber, saying, "I never was much good with handguns."

"Oh God," groaned Toby, rolling over onto his back. "Who the hell are you people?"

"Remember the girl?" asked Nati, stepping over him, pointing the Winchester directly at his head. "Remember the girl you raped?"

He shook his head, eyes screwed up with pain. "Girl? What…?" He stopped. "Jesus… you. You're the sister. And the priest…"

Ritter saw the memory making itself known through the piercing pain. Something changed in Toby's face. Agony turned to fear.

"I knew you'd remember," she said and shot him between the eyes.

Tying Up Loose Ends

After Reece's death, a long-drawn-out and particularly agonizing one, the Scrimshaw ranch, built up over the years by Silas, passed over to the single remaining claimant – Manuela. She, however, had disappeared, never to be heard of again. Some said she went south, into Texas, others that she went east, to New York, where she prospered.

Ritter was the benefactor now. After they escaped from El Paso and made their way north, he and Nati, together with Jeremiah, took over the running of the ranch and lived out their lives in peace.

Nobody pursued them and Doctor Wainright's full explanation of what happened seemed to satisfy everyone that the deaths of the cowhands and their boss was a matter of self-defence. Father Merry, however, remained in a chronic state until he died less than a week later.

Han returned to his island home of Okinawa, with his sister, Miyoko. Upon arriving at his village, he told those willing to listen that the fabled land of America was not the paradise everyone believed it to be; rather, it was a hard, unforgiving place, full of wicked, violent men whose only concern was the accumulation of money, through whatever means.

Susannah lived out her days in a sanatorium just outside the growing city of Salt Lake, Utah. There, she would decry anything Chinese and swear that at any moment her husband would return to take her home. Of course, this never happened. Within two years, she succumbed to typhoid fever and died alone and, for the most part, forgotten.

Lieutenant Connick did his utmost to discover the whereabouts of Captain Jewson, but to no avail. His investigations revealed the depth of the Captain's crimes, after a large metal box was discovered under the man's bed. Inside was a healthy sum of over fifteen thousand dollars, together with maps, half-finished notes scribbled hastily on stubs of paper, and a title deed to a plot of land over in Wyoming.

The lawyers acting on the Captain's behalf neither knew nor cared where the money to acquire the land had come from, but they informed Connick it would now be put into probate until such time as a relative could be found to take it over. None ever was, and the plot soon became overgrown until, many years later, it was sold by public auction to a syndicate of chicken farmers. It is still there. As to Connick, he died fighting the Apaches during the twilight of the Native Americans' struggle against the white man's oppression. Fittingly perhaps, it was a bullet from the great Geronimo that ended the officer's life.

It was to the town of Archangel that Francis returned, to receive a warm reception from the townsfolk and a far frostier one from his wife. He met up with Cable and Wilbur, to whom he recounted his escapades in great detail, and a telegram was sent to Cheyenne, calling for a second marshal to visit and investigate. As Marshal Climes' death was now treated as murder, the response of the U.S. authorities was swift. When it comes to looking after their own, they are quick to seek justice. The entire blame was laid at Reece Scrimshaw's door, but as he, along with everyone else of his clan, was now dead, the case was formally closed.

Francis lived out the rest of his days retelling stories of the bounty hunter Ritter and the strange, silent and deadly Okinawan who moved like the wind and killed with his bare hands.

He rarely mentioned his meeting with John Wesley Hardin.

Until, that is, at the ripe old age of eighty-six, he took to his horse for the last time and rode out to the sprawling Scrimshaw ranch. There, he met Gus Ritter, sitting on his porch as he so often did these days, and showed him the newspaper headlines. The story which followed brought Ritter no joy, only a sad acceptance of how cruel fate can be.

El Paso, 1895

On the morning it happened, John Wesley lay on his bed, still brooding over the recent argument he and his latest girlfriend, a firebrand widow by the name of M'ose McRose, had had the night before. They were both very drunk and the words they spat out were full of venom and designed to hurt. At some point, Hardin drifted off to sleep, fully-clothed. He woke up to find her gone. He swung his legs over the bed and stood up, rolling his tongue around the inside of his mouth. The taste he found there hovered somewhere between stale tobacco juice and horse sweat. Reaching for a nearby bottle, he cleansed his palette with a healthy slug of bourbon.

He checked her wardrobe in the small, cluttered hotel room they shared, and gained considerable relief from finding all her clothes still dangling from hangers, or folded neatly in various drawers. She had not left him, merely stormed out to find herself something to drink, no doubt.

Fourteen years of imprisonment and a qualification in law had done little to modify John Wesley Hardin's behavior. Found guilty of the manslaughter of Deputy Charles Webb, after defending himself with effective eloquence, he did his time quietly, thinking and repenting, promising himself that his former life of violence and gunplay was now squarely behind him.

It wasn't.

On his release, he made his way to the violent town of El Paso, but he soon fell in with bad company, shooting dice and playing cards whilst half-heartedly attempting to set himself up in the law profession. One of his first customers was M'ose, angry that one of her customers had short-changed her for services received. Hardin soon discovered what those particular services were when M'ose took something of a shine to him, telling him she particularly liked his great handlebar moustache, a sure sign, so she told him, of virility and expertise in bed. On their first night together, she screamed with genuine passion for one of the few times in her life and knew she had found her true love.

But their relationship was volatile, as underlined by that morning's outrages. She'd punched and kicked him and had now walked out, cursing his name. After drinking, he stepped out to find her.

He'd been in El Paso for a little over two weeks.

It was Bradley who first spotted him. Town ordinances demanded that guns of any kind should be handed into the sheriff's office upon arrival. With the guns occupying most of his attention, it wasn't until he made his way across the street towards where the man stood, that Bradley recognized him. He stopped short, a knot developing inside him, drawing tighter with every passing second. Unable to move, he gawped, not knowing what to do or say.

It was him! John Wesley Hardin, the one who'd left him to die out in the desert all those years ago. The man he'd sworn to kill.

Bradley burst through the office door, making John Selman jump, and fell into the nearest chair, head in hands, his fingers clawing at his scalp.

"What in the hell's the matter with you?"

"It's him," muttered Bradley from behind his hands, without looking up. He rocked backwards and forwards, his voice strained.

"Who?" Selman stepped up to his younger deputy. "Bradley, you're not making a whole lot of sense. Who are you—?"

"Hardin," said Bradley. He dropped his hands, revealing a tear-stained face. "He's here. I wanted to confront him, disarm him… I don't know *what* I wanted. But I couldn't. I couldn't do a thing. I was scared. Frightened to death. All these years I've spent with the hatred I feel for him festering inside me, and then, to see him…" He broke down again, sobbing even more loudly this time, totally inconsolable.

Selman took his time pouring out two hefty measures of bourbon from the bottle he always kept in his desk drawer. Without a word, he stuck one under Bradley's nose. "Drink it. Then we'll work out what to do."

What they worked out was to wait rather than immediately confront Hardin, as that would almost certainly lead to gunplay. They would then engineer a situation which would compromise the gunfighter and give the lawmen an excuse to act. Selman, too, had reasons for wanting Hardin out of the way. Past dealings meant he harboured a wealth of ill-feeling and longed for the chance to not only get his own back, but also enhance his own reputation as a gun-fighter. As things turned out, these reasons were not the main contributors to him seeking Hardin's demise.

The fateful day was the one in which M'ose stormed out from their small, cluttered hotel room, furious about Hardin's insistence that she should let him sleep and quit groping at his groin. M'ose, a physically demanding girl, had taken this rejection as a personal slight. Temper frayed and sexual frustration rising, she trawled through several saloons, drinking hard and fast and flashing come-on smiles to any number of patrons, most of whom responded to her smouldering look, her slim waist, her long, raven-coloured hair, but most of all her full, soft mouth and the way she ran her tongue slowly and seductively along her bottom lip.

Enjoying the urgent whispers and the occasional hand slipping under her dress, she entertained two young men behind the Regal Hotel, taking all they had and leaving them gasping on the ground. One had a concealed Derringer in his jacket pocket. She deftly removed it and wandered into the street, waving it high above her head.

The first shot she fired caused onlookers to cheer and laugh.

The second prompted John Selman Junior to stride across the street, grip her by the wrist and twist the small pistol from her long, tapered fingers.

"You bastard!" she screeched. The stink of whisky on her breath caused Selman to recoil, giving her enough leverage to swing her knee up into his groin. He yelped and dropped to his knees, face creased up in agony.

Onlookers applauded. This was better than the burlesque show that ran twice-nightly on Friday and Saturday evenings down at the Pullman Theatre.

M'ose lapped it up, bowing theatrically with a wide flourish of her right hand. With her back turned to the lawman, she didn't notice Selman had recovered sufficiently to get to his feet. All at once, she felt herself being yanked backwards by her hair. With spittle spraying from his gritted teeth, Selman grated, "You're under arrest, you bitch!"

Having learnt her self-defence lessons well, and ignoring the pain from her pulled hair, M'ose clamped her hand over his, pressed it hard against her head, twisted in his grip and rammed her other fist into his solar plexus. The air exploded from his mouth and he released his hold. She jabbed the point of her high-heeled boot into his shin with a fearful crack and flounced away, brandishing the Derringer, whooping with glee. The assembled crowd cheered.

And then Hardin appeared.

The commotion beneath his window had roused him from his drunken sleep and when he looked out into the street and saw M'ose, he snatched his gun belt from where it hung on the end of his bed and raced downstairs.

Selman was just clambering to his feet for a second time, disorientated and gasping with pain, when Hardin loomed across his field of vision and pistol-whipped him across the side of the head, dumping him unconscious onto the ground.

"You're coming back with me," said Hardin, catching up with M'ose as she swayed uncertainly outside the Acme saloon.

"The hell I am!" she said and turned, pointing the Derringer at his face. "Touch me and I'll blow your damned head off."

"Not if it ain't loaded," he said and wrestled the gun from her hand. He then back-slapped her across the face and she fell onto her backside and burst into tears. Reaching down, he took her by the hand and led her inside.

A few whiskies later, she was fully recovered and happy to sit in the corner and drink herself into unconsciousness whilst Hardin partook of a quiet game of dice with some out-of-towners.

"That's nasty," said Bradley, dipping a corner of his neckerchief into a glass of bourbon and dabbing it into the open wound above John Junior's left eye.

Selman gave a shriek. "*Jesus*, Brad, take it easy!"

"Hold your horses, you damn pansy," laughed Bradley, doing his best to clean away the blood. "This'll only take but a minute."

"Damn it all, she was like a wildcat."

"Yes, she has a certain reputation," Bradley said, applying more bourbon. "Why in hell didn't you just leave her be?"

"She was shooting off that Derringer and Pa insists we enforce his law, come what may." He gave Bradley a hard look. "Not that you did so with Hardin."

"Hell, Johnny, would you?" Bradley shook his head, picked up what was left of the bourbon and swallowed it down. "He makes M'ose seem like a pussycat."

"He can't get away with what he done. Not out in the street, in front of everyone."

"No. You're right. I guess John will have something to say about it all."

At that moment, the door swung open and John Selman Senior strode in, face like thunder, jowls red, eyes wide, breathing so hard he was snorting like a bull. "Damned right I have something to say about it. What in hell happened out there, boy?"

John Selman Junior cowered under his father's rage. Not daring to look into his eyes, he managed a whimpering, "I'm sorry, Pa."

"First, that hot-headed whore slaps you down, then Hardin finishes the job." He pushed Bradley aside and helped himself to a measure of bourbon. "This might, however, be the silver lining we've been waiting for, Brad."

Frowning, the deputy looked from son to father. "Meaning…?"

"Meaning you go over to the Acme and engage that bastard in conversation. Keep him occupied and allow me the edge I need against him."

"How am I supposed to do that?"

"Any goddamned way you please! Hell, Bradley, he left you for dead out in the wilderness. Confront him, tell him you've come to pay him back for what he done."

"Hell, he won't remember that."

"Of course he will! Damn it all, he would have shot you dead if it would have given him more pleasure. Tell him you want revenge, call him out, but keep his attention on you whilst I get myself in a position to better him."

"*Better* him?" said John Selman Junior, touching the seeping wound next to his eye. "What you planning on doing, Pa?"

"I'm gonna kill the bastard."

Hardin did not look up from his dice game when Bradley sauntered into the Acme Saloon not ten minutes after his conversation with John Selman. The place was buzzing with activity. Late afternoon, customers already well-oiled with whisky and beer, raucous laughter mingled with the tinny sound of an out-of-tune piano situated under the main staircase – a staircase upon which lounged three brightly-painted whores, eager for custom.

Ordering a drink, Bradley leant his back against the counter and allowed his eyes to scan the room. Not half a dozen paces away, Hardin stood, shirt-sleeves rolled up, a thin film of sweat across his brow, dark patches under his arms, the brace of pistols displayed in brazen, open contempt for the law. He stood side-on to Bradley, facing the main door, but with his full attention fixed on the dice he sent rolling across the green baize.

He threw back his head and laughed when he made the score he needed, and emptied his glass in one. Turning his head to the bar as he prepared to shout an order for another drink, he intercepted Bradley's hard stare and, for a moment, something like a flash of recognition crossed his face. But then it was gone. "Whisky, Pat!"

The barkeep dutifully poured out a full measure but, before he could carry the drink over, Bradley picked up the glass. "Allow me," he said, with a broad grin.

Placing the glass in front of the gunfighter, Bradley stepped back, opening his frock-coat to reveal his Colt revolver at his hip and his badge of office pinned to his chest.

A hush descended on the small group of dice-players. It soon spread until the entire room fell into an expectant hush. The piano ceased. A heaviness developed in the air and Bradley saw Hardin pause and look. Fear hit him then, like a living thing slithering through his guts and he suddenly became aware of the precariousness of his situation.

"Do I know you?"

Trying hard not to swallow, Bradley fought against an overwhelming desire to flee. Forcing his mind back to that fateful day when Hardin abandoned him to almost certain death, he tipped his head forward slightly and, unblinking, stared into the gunfighter's face. "You should."

Several patrons, deeming their proximity to the two men as far too dangerous, edged away. Hardin nodded towards Bradley's star. "Can't say I do, Deputy."

"Nigh on fifteen years ago it was. Fate brought us together."

The main entrance door creaked open. Nobody flinched.

"Fifteen years is a long time, Deputy. I've been kinda busy since then."

"We talked about a friend of mine. His family."

"Still nothing. Deputy, you seem a tad anxious. Mind telling me what it is that is troubling you?"

"You saved me from a fat guy who wanted to blow my head off. Then, when I told you about what happened to my friend and his family, you got upset. Remember that?"

"Like I said, nothing comes to mind. Maybe you've got the wrong person?"

"No. It was you." He leaned forward. A figure slipped through the press of people who were watching this tense exchange. Bradley forced a smile. "My friend's family was attacked, but their farmhand helped them. He was black."

Something stopped. Not only time and space, but Hardin's breathing. His eyes narrowed.

Damn him to hell, he remembers.

"And as you hate black folk so much, you took exception to what I said. You took exception to *me*, damn your soul to hell."

"I left you for dead," hissed Hardin, stepping clear of the table, "and that was a grave mistake to make, I see that now."

"The fates have conspired against you, and now you're going to pay."

"Am I?" He cocked his head. "Then why not make your demand?"

They stared into one another's eyes, emotions poised. The silence pressed in.

"Give up your weapons, John Wesley Hardin," boomed a voice, shattering the preternatural stillness of the room.

Hardin frowned, for it was not the man in front of him who had spoken, but someone from behind.

Too late, he whirled, hand springing for his gun, and the bullet exploded in the back of his head, pitching him against the table edge, from which he bounced and fell to the floor.

Bradley staggered away, hand against his mouth, unable to believe that he still drew breath. He watched John Selman stepping over the prone figure of the gunfighter and put three more bullets into his chest.

John Wesley Hardin lay dead, but even then his hand had managed to pull out his gun from its holster.

"That's quite a story," said Ritter quietly, folding the newspaper in two and placing it on the small table beside him.

"I thought you might want to read it," said Francis. "Selman himself was gunned down just a few weeks later. Bradley, his deputy, handed in his badge soon after. Went off into the Indian Territories, so it is said."

Nodding, Ritter gazed across the sprawling ranchland before him. "I wanted to kill him so much," he said quietly.

"That's understandable. You thought he'd wronged you by killing your brother."

"But he hadn't." Riiter raised his head. "He'd tried to save him. If it wasn't for you..."

Francis shrugged. "Fate, I guess. But anyways, to kill a man is a hell of a thing."

"Yes, it is. And it is something I have done often, but this one," he tapped the newspaper, "I am glad it was not me. Hardin did not deserve to die like that, shot in the back."

Nati, emerging from the interior of the house, acknowledged Francis with a fleeting smile, then went over to Ritter and pressed her hand gently on his shoulder. "You've had news?" He nodded. "Is it over?"

"Yes, it is." He turned, smiled, and settled his cheek on her hand. "And now at last I can rest easy."

Francis, standing there quietly, wondered if any of them would ever 'rest easy' again.

The End.

About the Author

Stuart G Yates is the author of a eclectic mix of books, ranging from historical fiction through to contemporary thrillers. Hailing from Merseyside, he now lives in southern Spain, where he teaches history, but dreams of living on a narrowboat in Shropshire.